EOD SOLDIERS

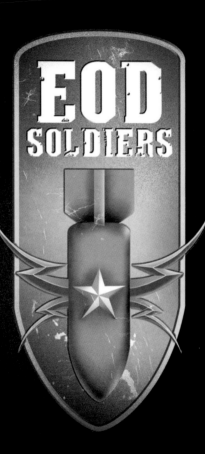

ne Arch Books,

1710 Roe Crest Drive
North Mankato, Minnesota 56003
www.mycapstone.com

Text and illustrations © 2017 Stone Arch Books

Library of Congress Cataloging-in-Publication Data is
available on the Library of Congress website.

ISBN: 978-1-4965-3109-4 (library binding)
ISBN: 978-1-4965-3113-1 (eBook PDF)

Summary: When she was just a kid, Rose Campbell's
father constantly told her to "take things slow." Now, as
an Explosive Ordnance Disposal Specialist, Rose takes
his advice to heart. One misstep, and boom — somebody
dies. But lately, every day feels exactly the same: IEDs
are placed in the same locations. Rose's team finds the
bombs and disarms them. Then they move on to the
next ones. No matter what, Rose must fight the urge to
grow impatient — because that's exactly what the bomb
makers are hoping for.

Designer: Brann Garvey

Printed in the United States of America.
009620F16

GO
SLOW

written by Matthew K. Manning
art by Carlos Furuzono and Dijjo Lima

STONE ARCH BOOKS
a capstone imprint

EOD
SOLDIERS

SPECIALIST ROSE CAMPBELL:

Rose Campbell is a no-nonsense soldier who is extremely proud of her position in the military.

ROSE CAMPBELL'S FATHER:

Campbell's father is a protective parent who hopes to impart the lessons he's learned in life to his daughter.

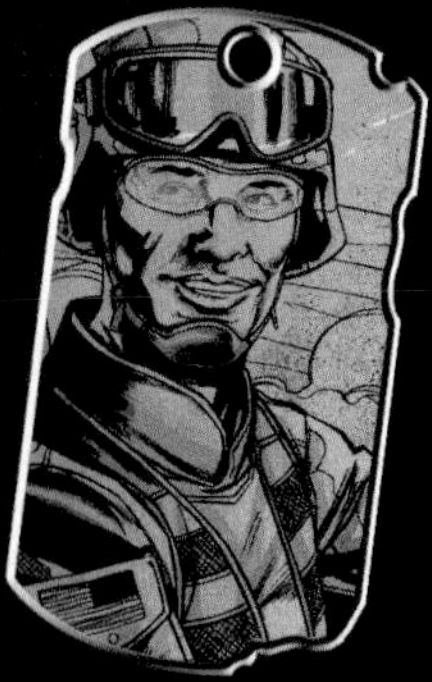

PRIVATE JASON ROGERS:

Rogers draws others in with his easy-going personality and contagious smile.

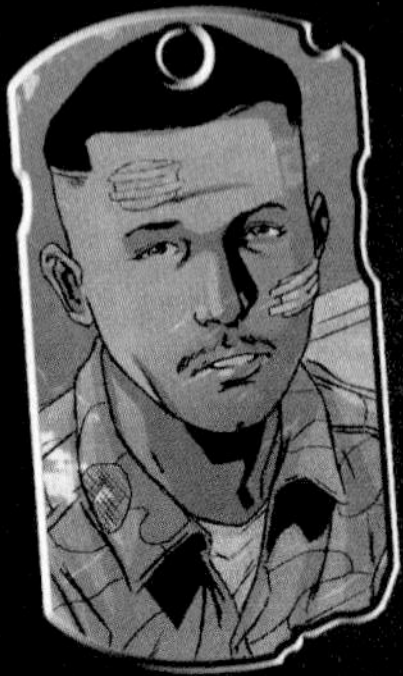

PRIVATE ELI RECATO:

Recato is a private of Filipino descent who grew up in the Midwest. As his rank indicates, Recato is a pretty fresh face to combat.

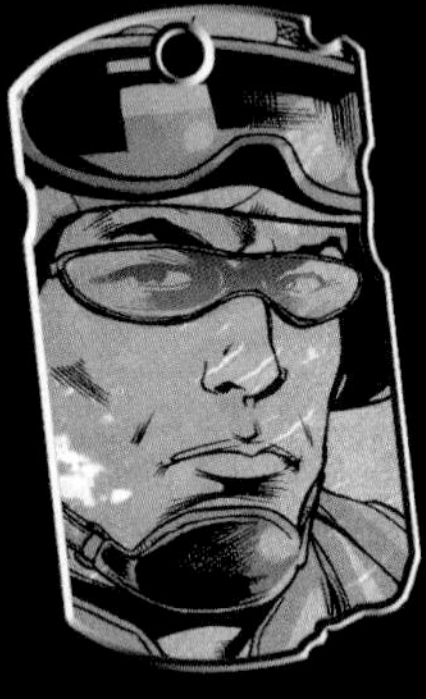

PRIVATE TOMMY BADGER:

Badger is a quintessential all-American type, but has a chip on his shoulder the size of a conjoined twin.

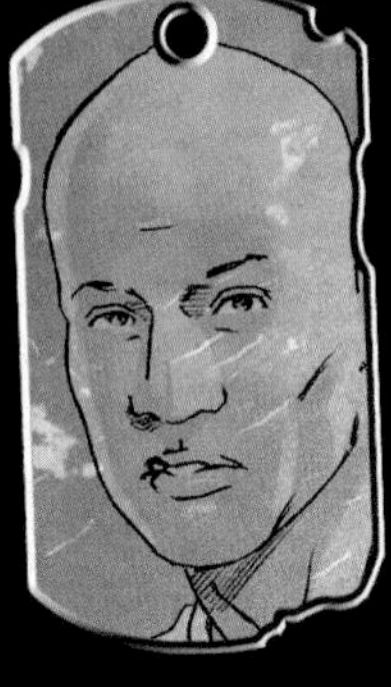

LIEUTENANT (LT) BRANCH:

As the commanding officer of their road-clearing crew, Branch is a tough leader with an even tougher demeanor.

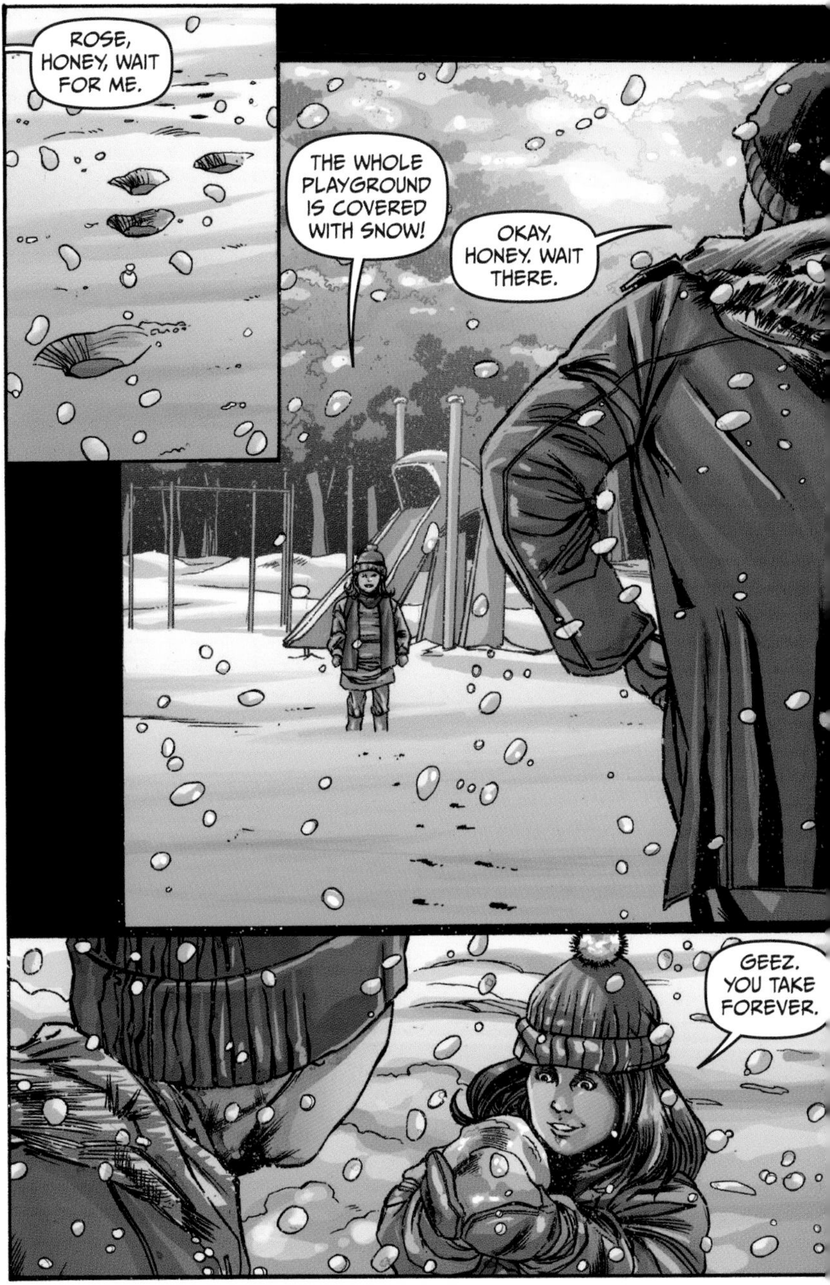
ROSE, HONEY, WAIT FOR ME.
THE WHOLE PLAYGROUND IS COVERED WITH SNOW!
OKAY, HONEY. WAIT THERE.
GEEZ. YOU TAKE FOREVER.

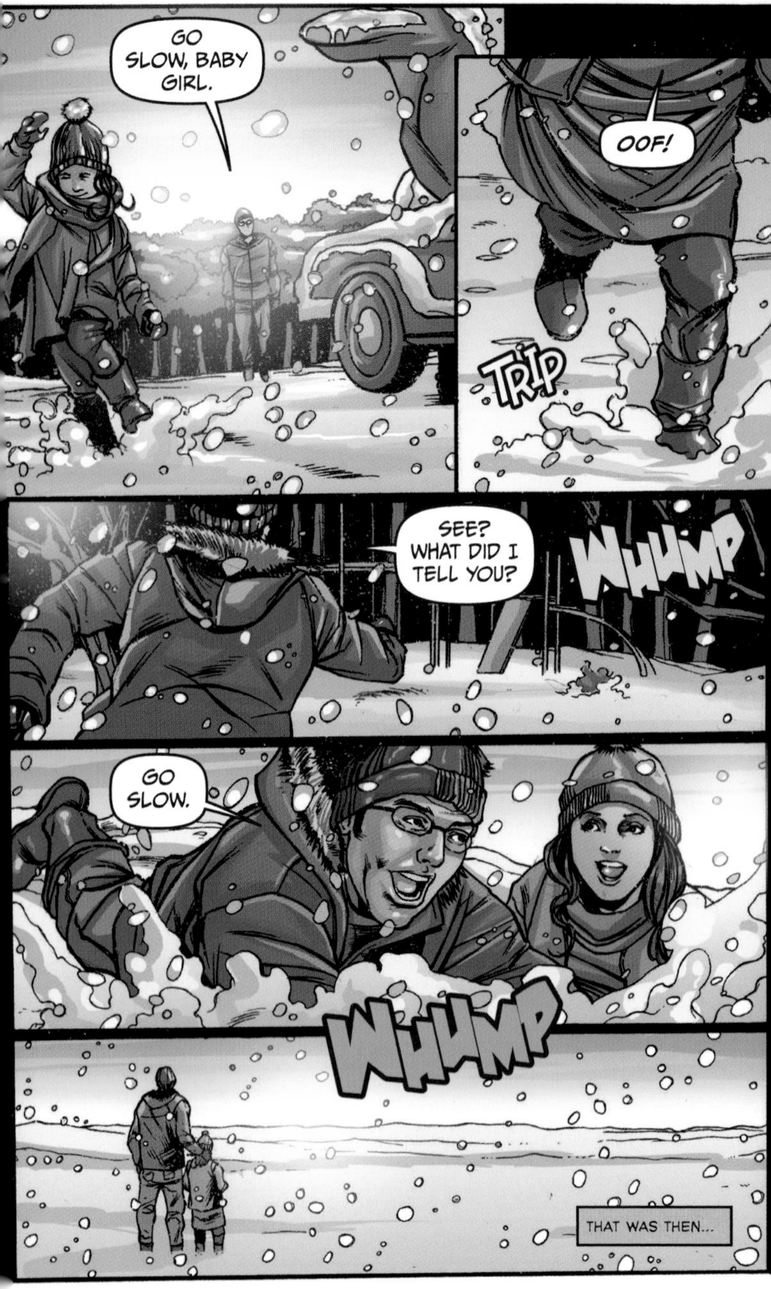
GO SLOW, BABY GIRL.
OOF!
TRIP
SEE? WHAT DID I TELL YOU?
WHUMP
GO SLOW.
WHUMP
THAT WAS THEN...

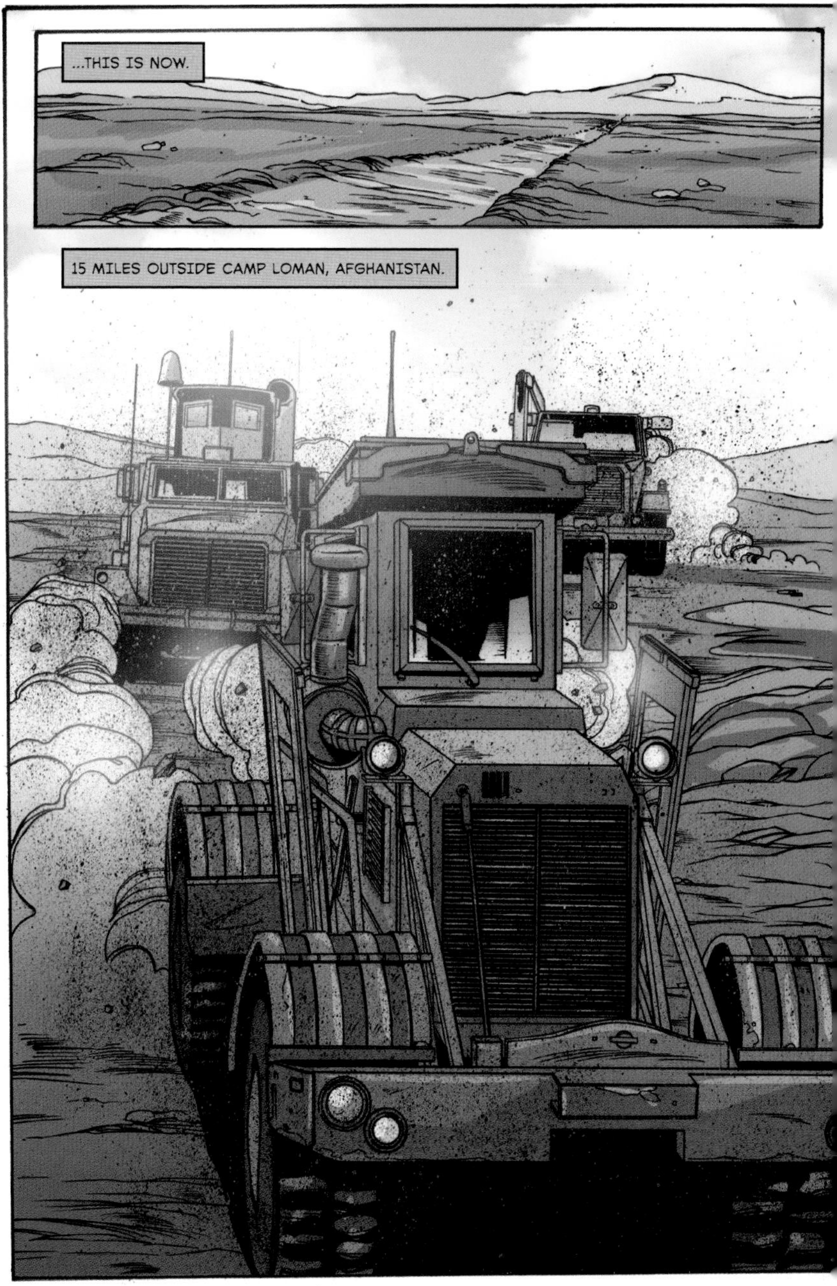
...THIS IS NOW.
15 MILES OUTSIDE CAMP LOMAN, AFGHANISTAN.

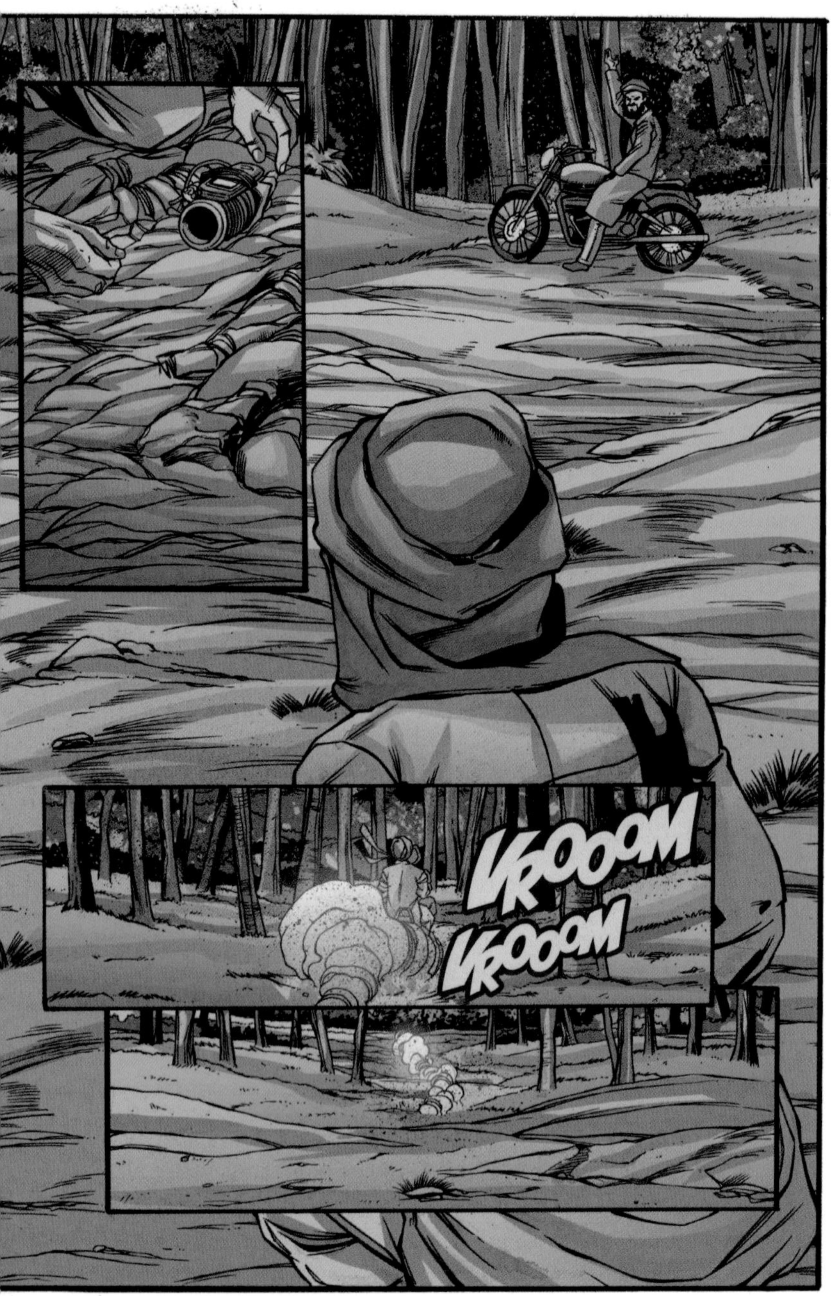
VROOOM
VROOOM

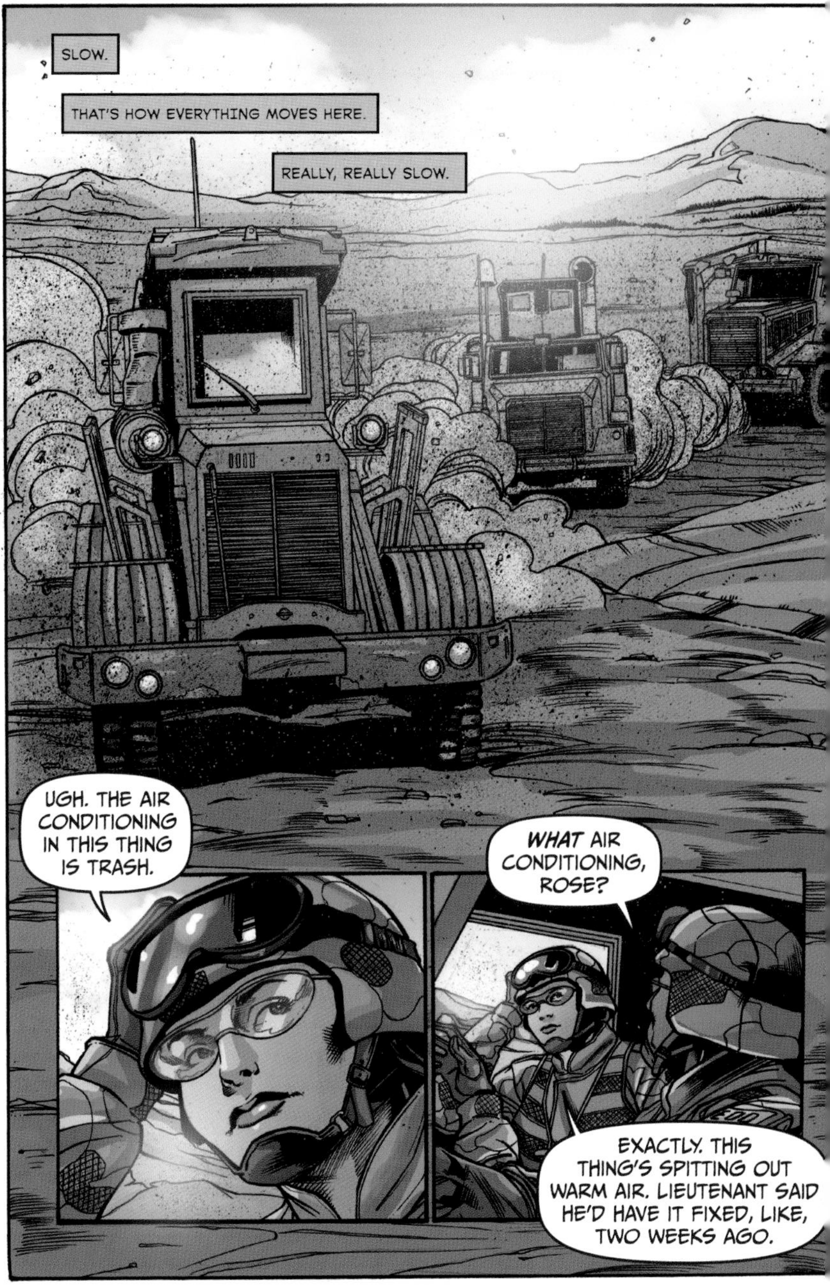
SLOW.
THAT'S HOW EVERYTHING MOVES HERE.
REALLY, REALLY SLOW.
UGH. THE AIR CONDITIONING IN THIS THING IS TRASH.
WHAT AIR CONDITIONING, ROSE?
EXACTLY. THIS THING'S SPITTING OUT WARM AIR. LIEUTENANT SAID HE'D HAVE IT FIXED, LIKE, TWO WEEKS AGO.

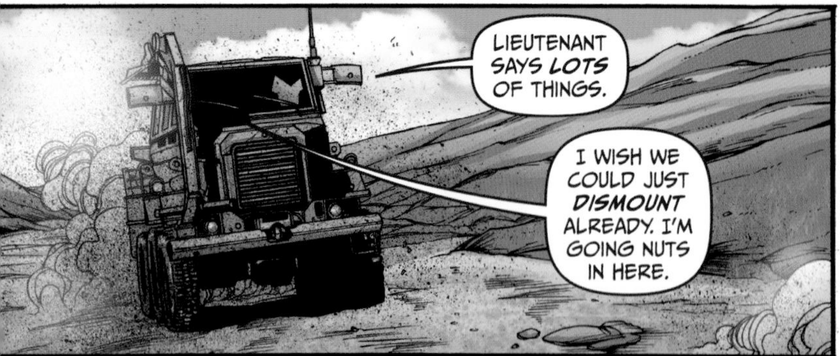
LIEUTENANT SAYS LOTS OF THINGS.
I WISH WE COULD JUST DISMOUNT ALREADY. I'M GOING NUTS IN HERE.

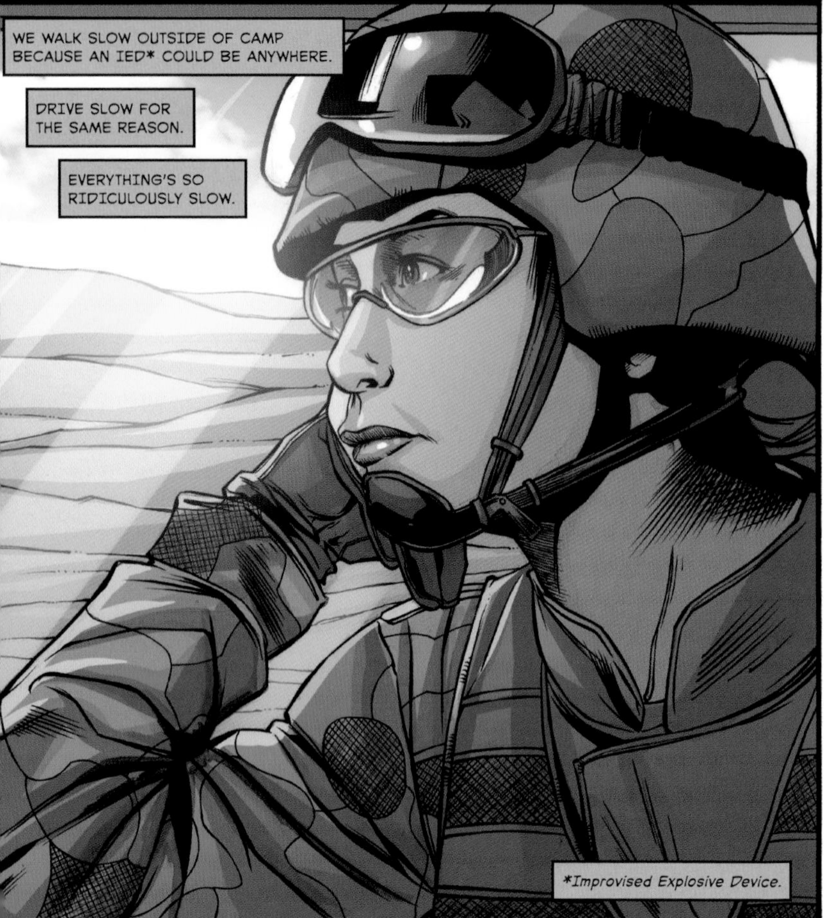
WE WALK SLOW OUTSIDE OF CAMP BECAUSE AN IED* COULD BE ANYWHERE.
DRIVE SLOW FOR THE SAME REASON.
EVERYTHING'S SO RIDICULOUSLY SLOW.
*Improvised Explosive Device.

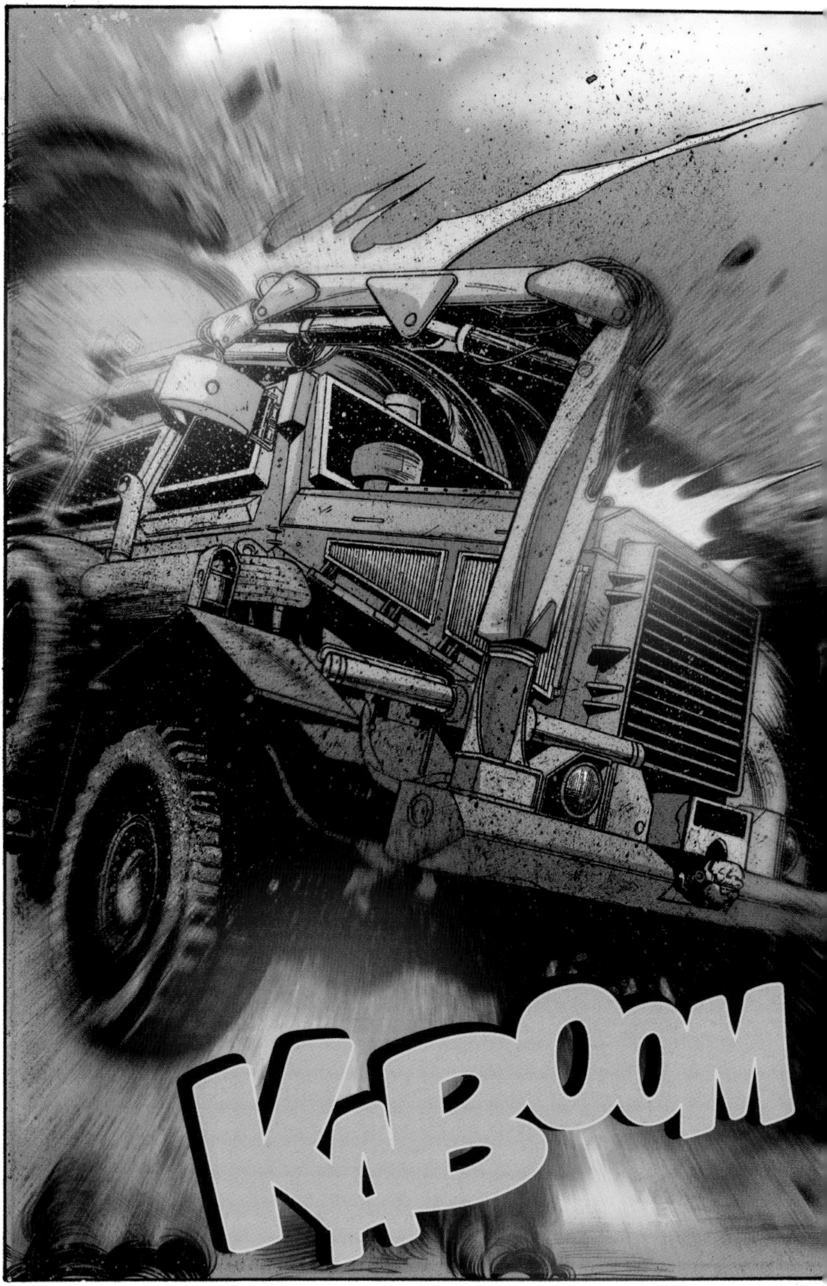
KABOOM

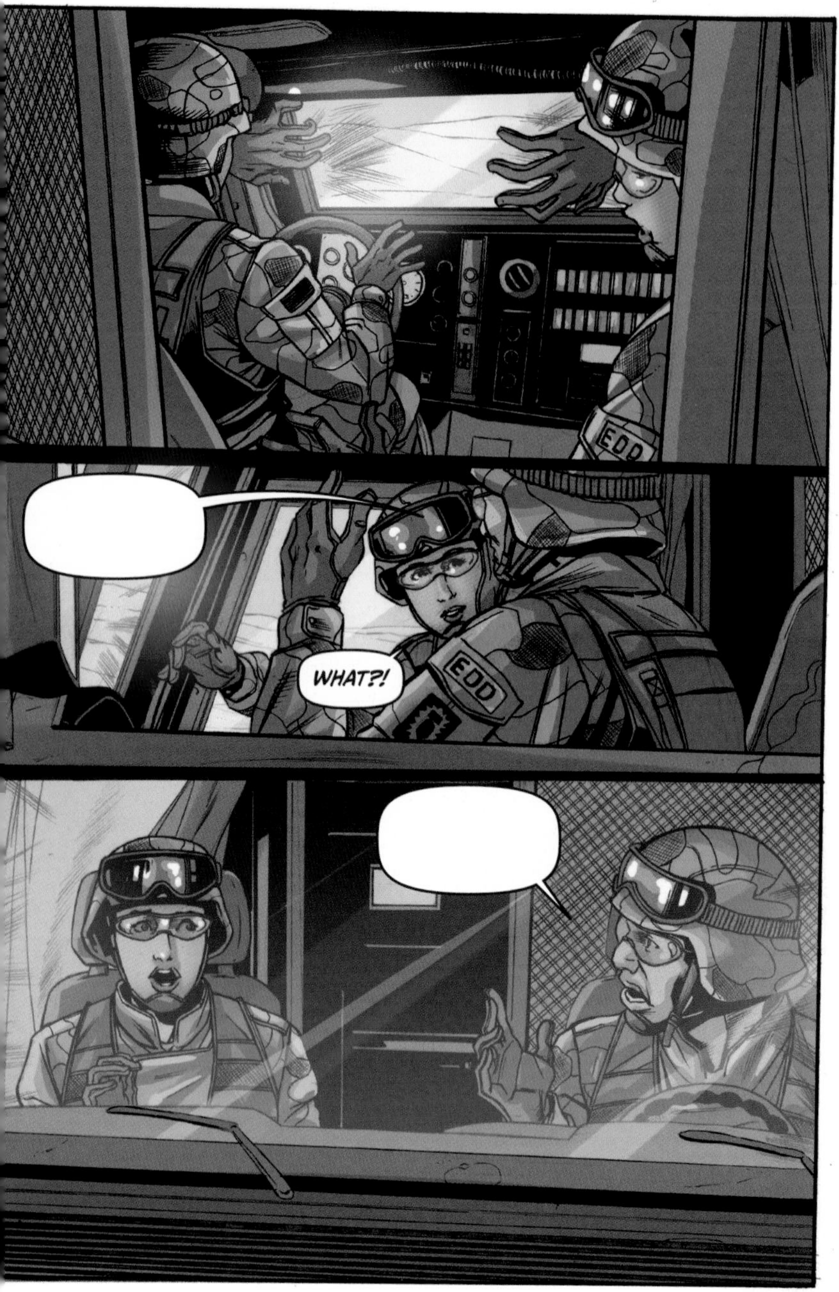
WHAT?!

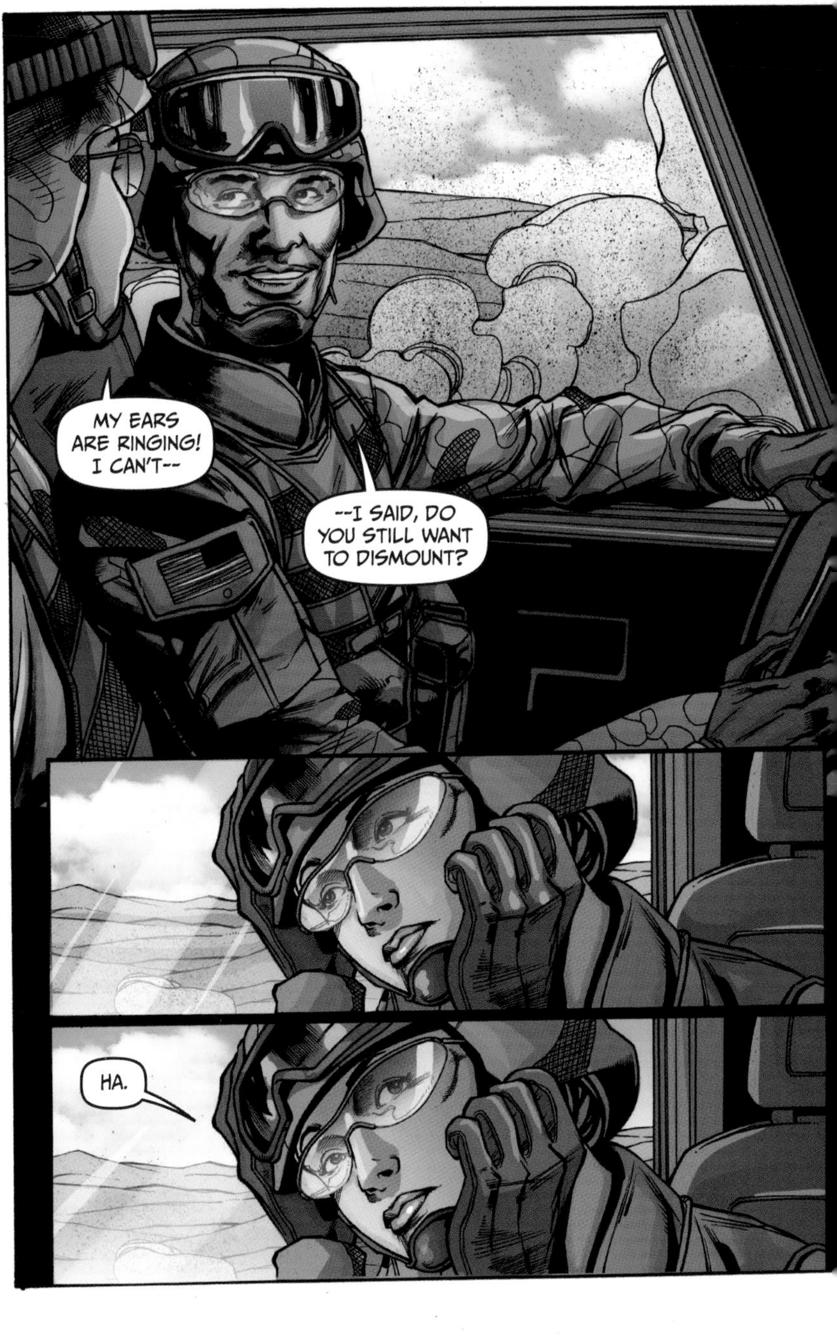
MY EARS ARE RINGING! I CAN'T--
--I SAID, DO YOU STILL WANT TO DISMOUNT?
HA.

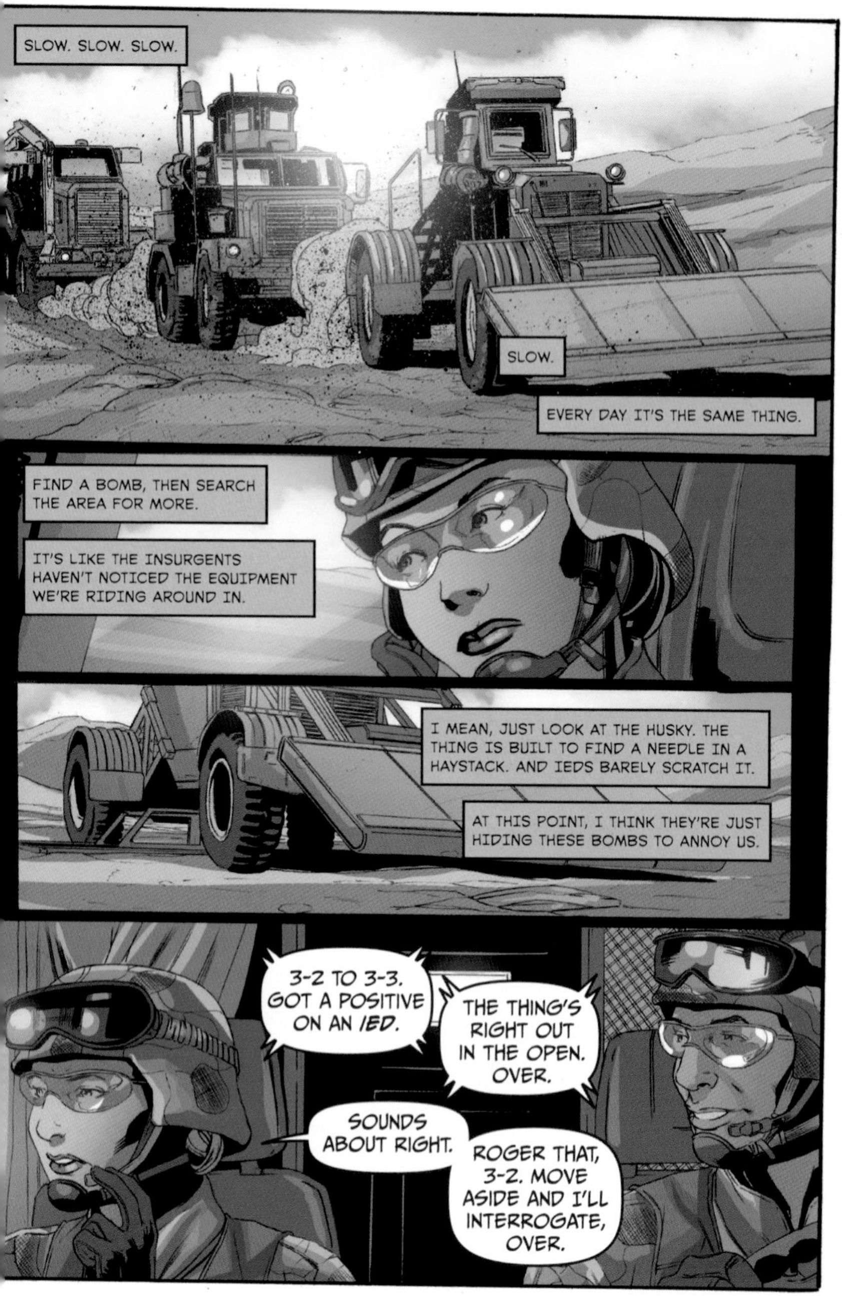
SLOW. SLOW. SLOW.
SLOW.
EVERY DAY IT'S THE SAME THING.
FIND A BOMB, THEN SEARCH THE AREA FOR MORE.
IT'S LIKE THE INSURGENTS HAVEN'T NOTICED THE EQUIPMENT WE'RE RIDING AROUND IN.
I MEAN, JUST LOOK AT THE HUSKY. THE THING IS BUILT TO FIND A NEEDLE IN A HAYSTACK. AND IEDS BARELY SCRATCH IT.
AT THIS POINT, I THINK THEY'RE JUST HIDING THESE BOMBS TO ANNOY US.
3-2 TO 3-3. GOT A POSITIVE ON AN *IED*.
THE THING'S RIGHT OUT IN THE OPEN. OVER.
SOUNDS ABOUT RIGHT.
ROGER THAT, 3-2. MOVE ASIDE AND I'LL INTERROGATE, OVER.

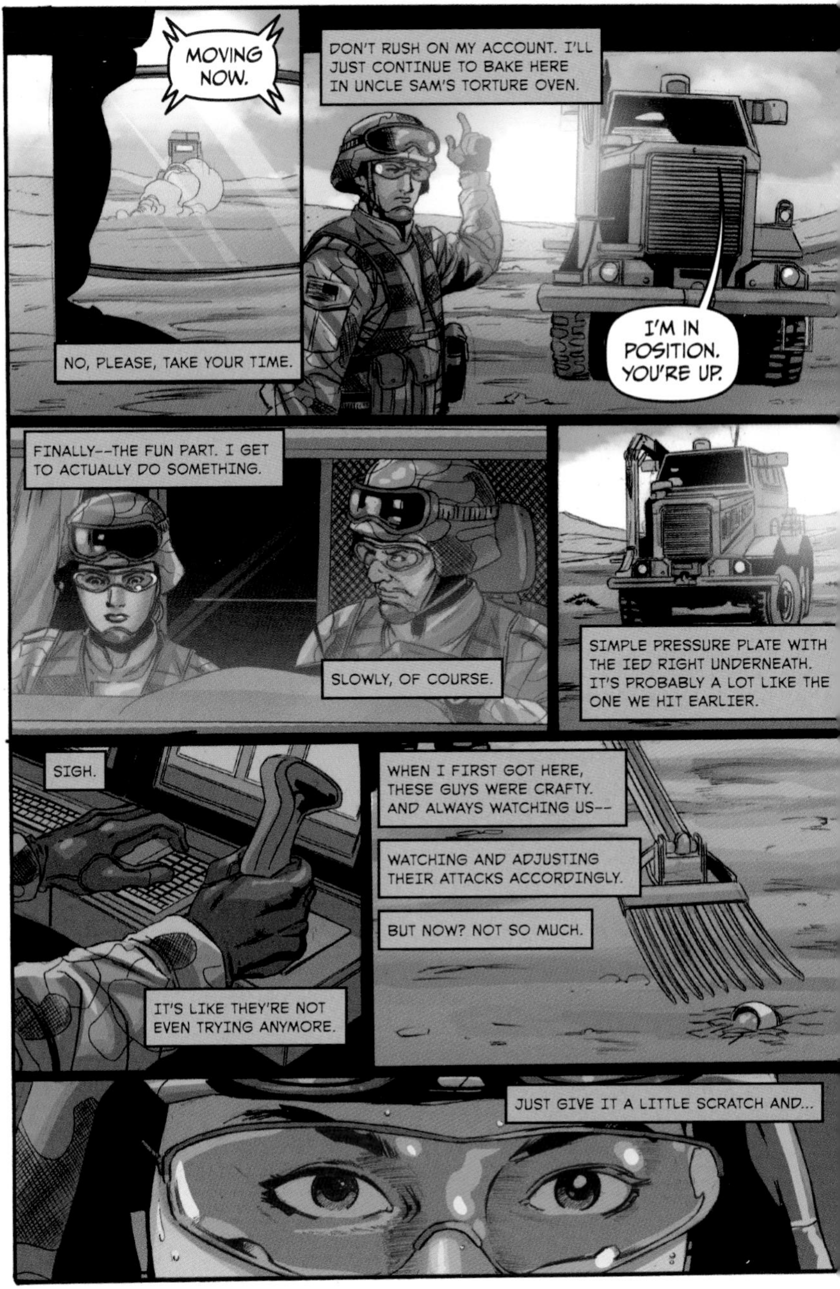
MOVING NOW.
NO, PLEASE, TAKE YOUR TIME.
DON'T RUSH ON MY ACCOUNT. I'LL JUST CONTINUE TO BAKE HERE IN UNCLE SAM'S TORTURE OVEN.
I'M IN POSITION. YOU'RE UP.
FINALLY--THE FUN PART. I GET TO ACTUALLY DO SOMETHING.
SLOWLY, OF COURSE.
SIMPLE PRESSURE PLATE WITH THE IED RIGHT UNDERNEATH. IT'S PROBABLY A LOT LIKE THE ONE WE HIT EARLIER.
SIGH.
IT'S LIKE THEY'RE NOT EVEN TRYING ANYMORE.
WHEN I FIRST GOT HERE, THESE GUYS WERE CRAFTY. AND ALWAYS WATCHING US--
WATCHING AND ADJUSTING THEIR ATTACKS ACCORDINGLY.
BUT NOW? NOT SO MUCH.
JUST GIVE IT A LITTLE SCRATCH AND...

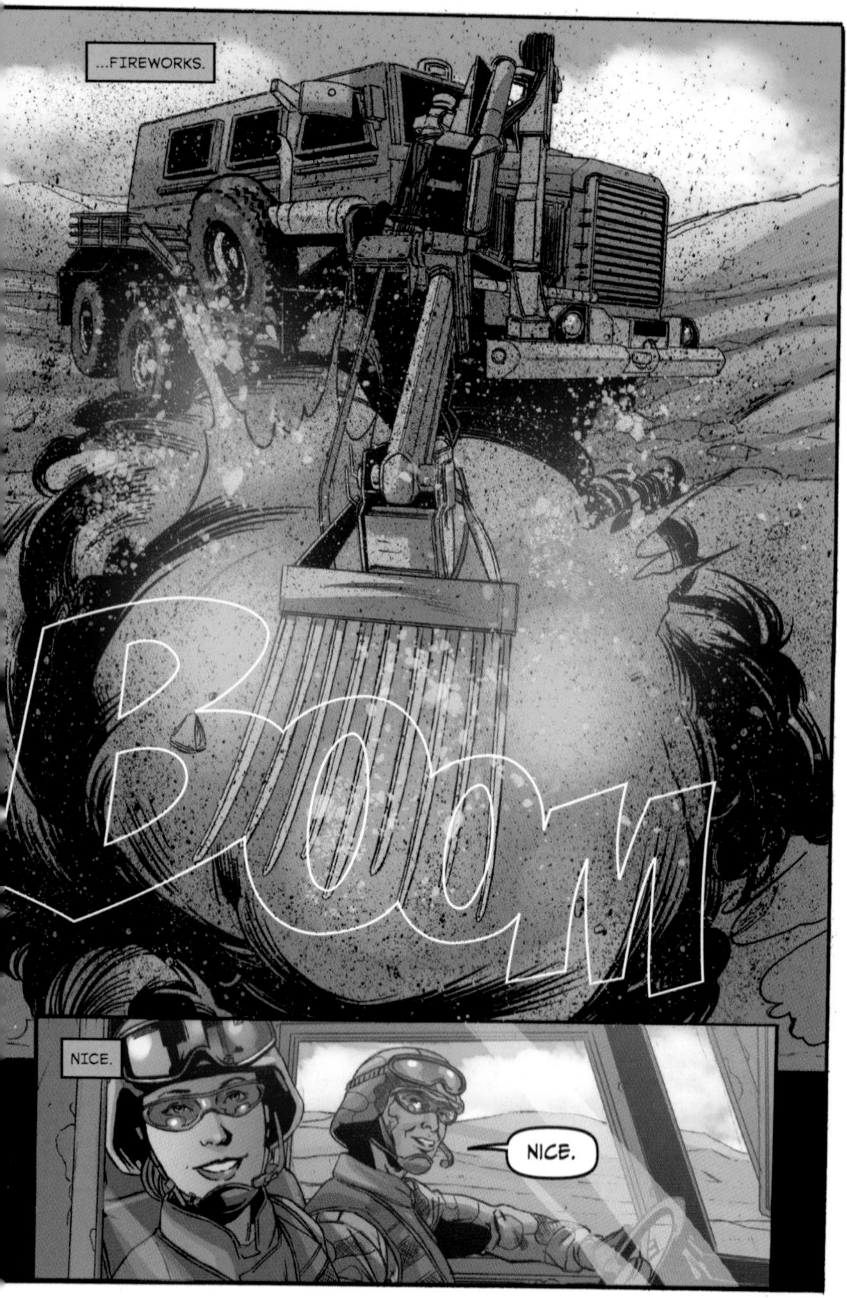
...FIREWORKS.
BOOM
NICE.
NICE.

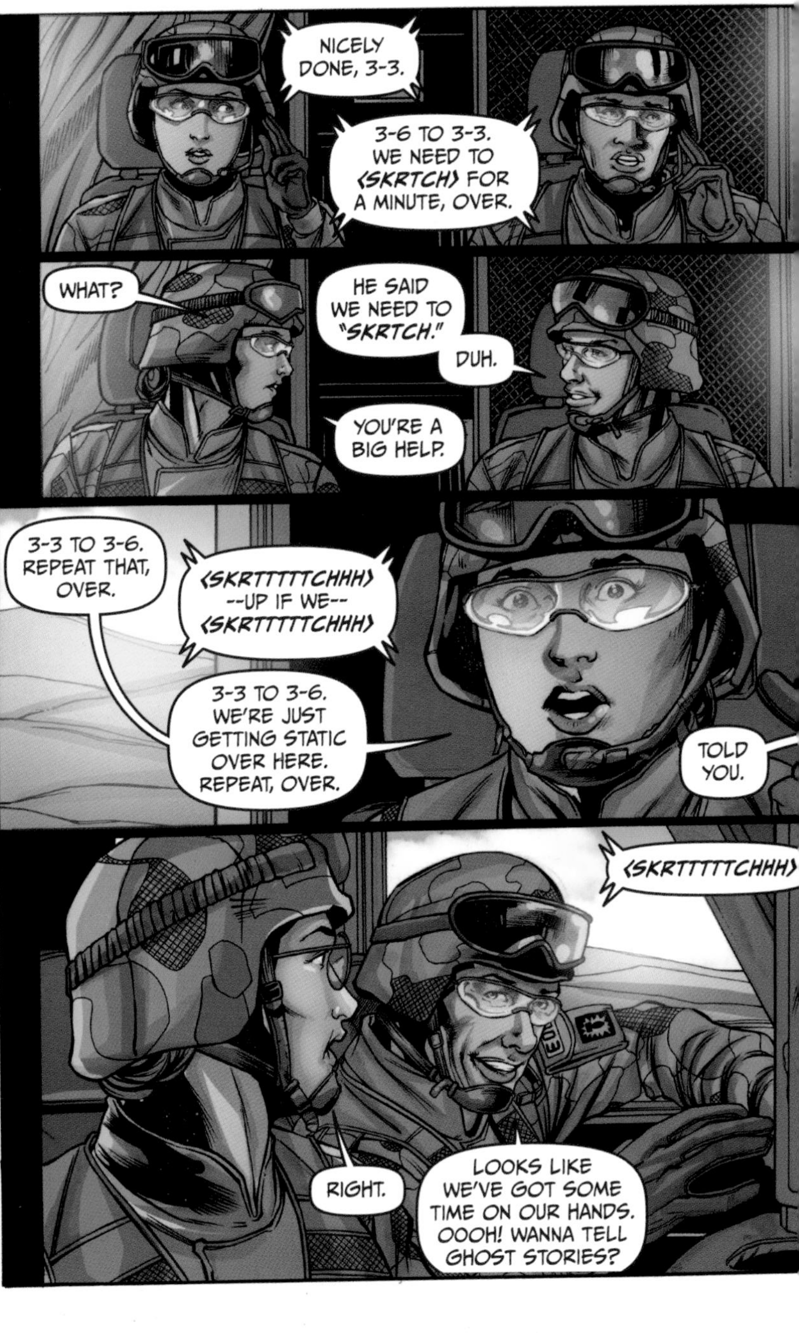
NICELY DONE, 3-3.
3-6 TO 3-3. WE NEED TO ⟨SKRTCH⟩ FOR A MINUTE, OVER.
WHAT?
HE SAID WE NEED TO "SKRTCH."
DUH.
YOU'RE A BIG HELP.
3-3 TO 3-6. REPEAT THAT, OVER.
⟨SKRTTTTTCHHH⟩ --UP IF WE-- ⟨SKRTTTTTCHHH⟩
3-3 TO 3-6. WE'RE JUST GETTING STATIC OVER HERE. REPEAT, OVER.
TOLD YOU.
⟨SKRTTTTTCHHH⟩
RIGHT.
LOOKS LIKE WE'VE GOT SOME TIME ON OUR HANDS. OOOH! WANNA TELL GHOST STORIES?

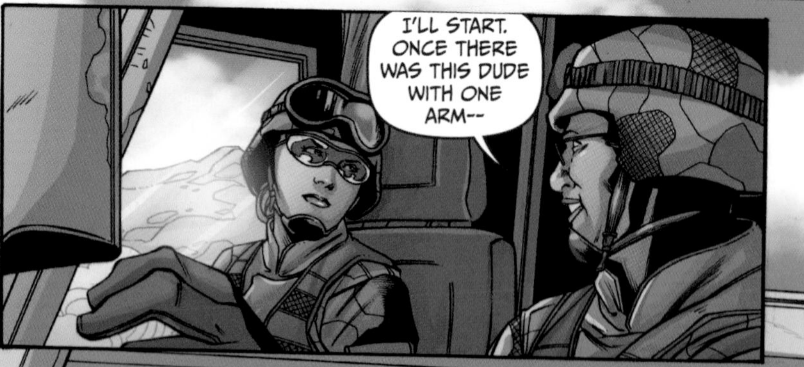
I'LL START. ONCE THERE WAS THIS DUDE WITH ONE ARM--

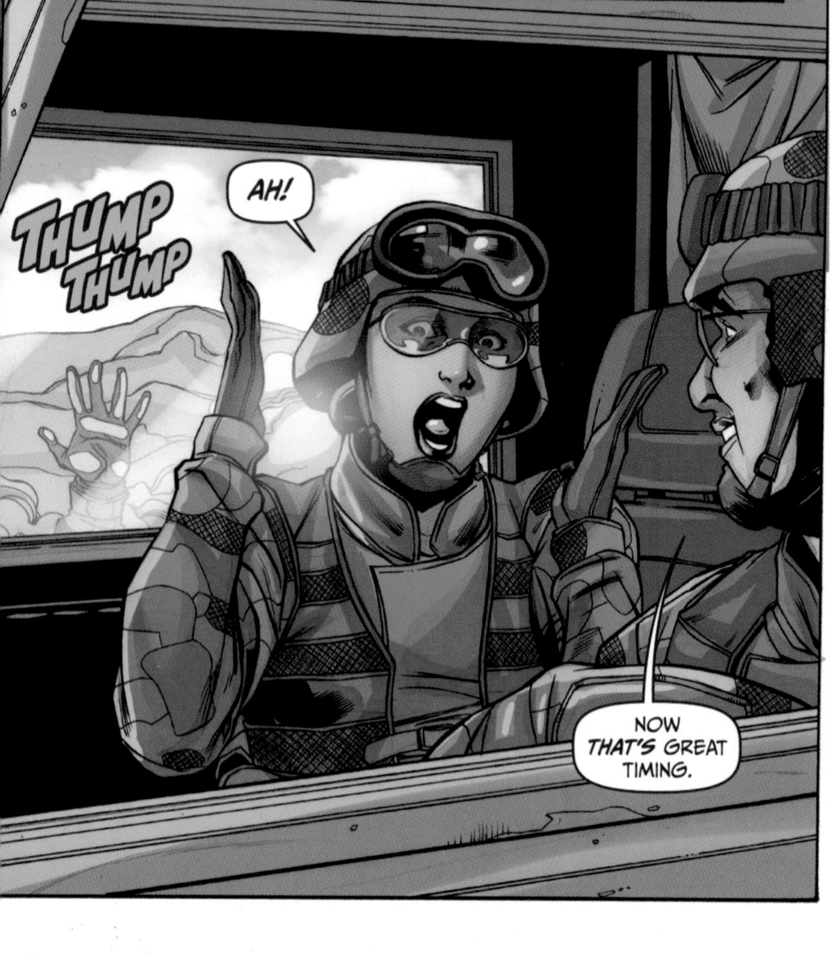
THUMP THUMP
AH!
NOW THAT'S GREAT TIMING.

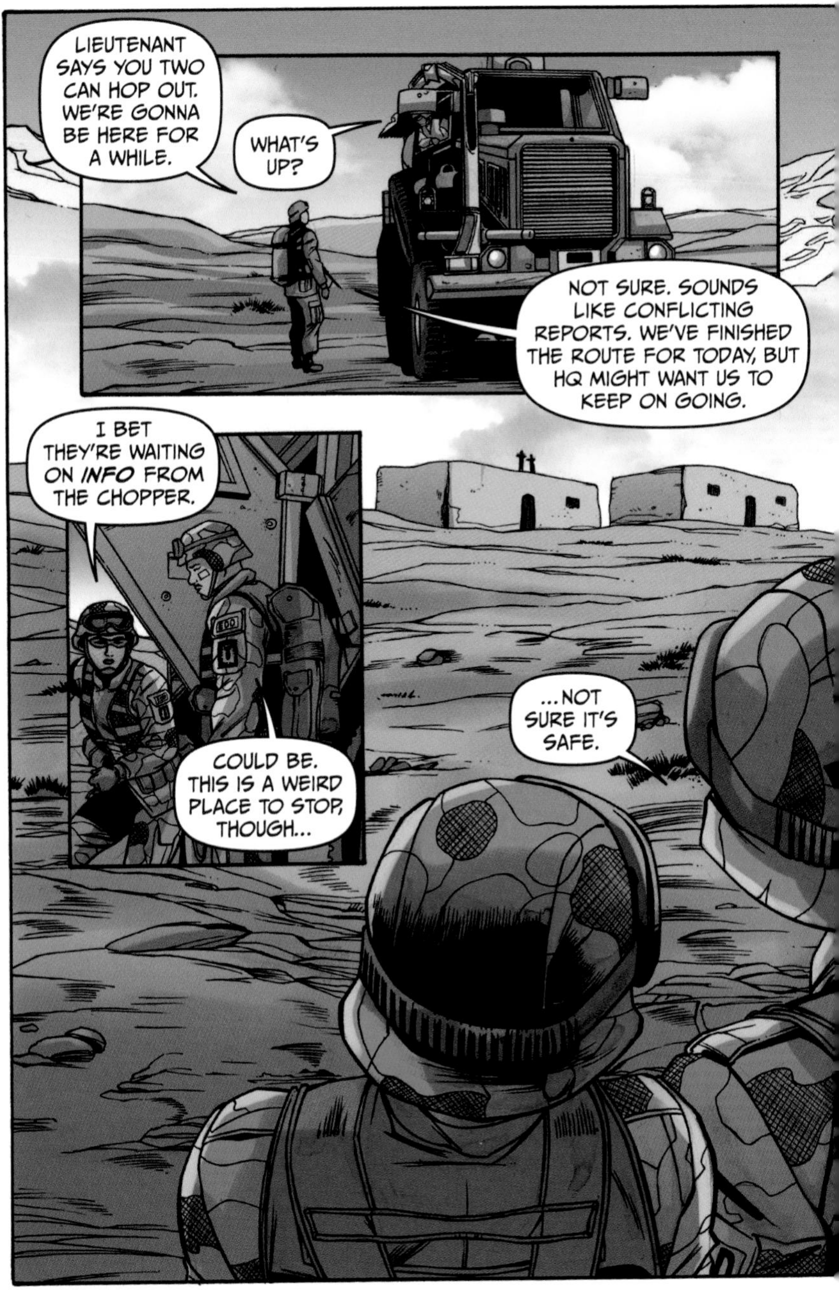
LIEUTENANT SAYS YOU TWO CAN HOP OUT. WE'RE GONNA BE HERE FOR A WHILE.
WHAT'S UP?
NOT SURE. SOUNDS LIKE CONFLICTING REPORTS. WE'VE FINISHED THE ROUTE FOR TODAY, BUT HQ MIGHT WANT US TO KEEP ON GOING.
I BET THEY'RE WAITING ON *INFO* FROM THE CHOPPER.
COULD BE. THIS IS A WEIRD PLACE TO STOP, THOUGH...
...NOT SURE IT'S SAFE.

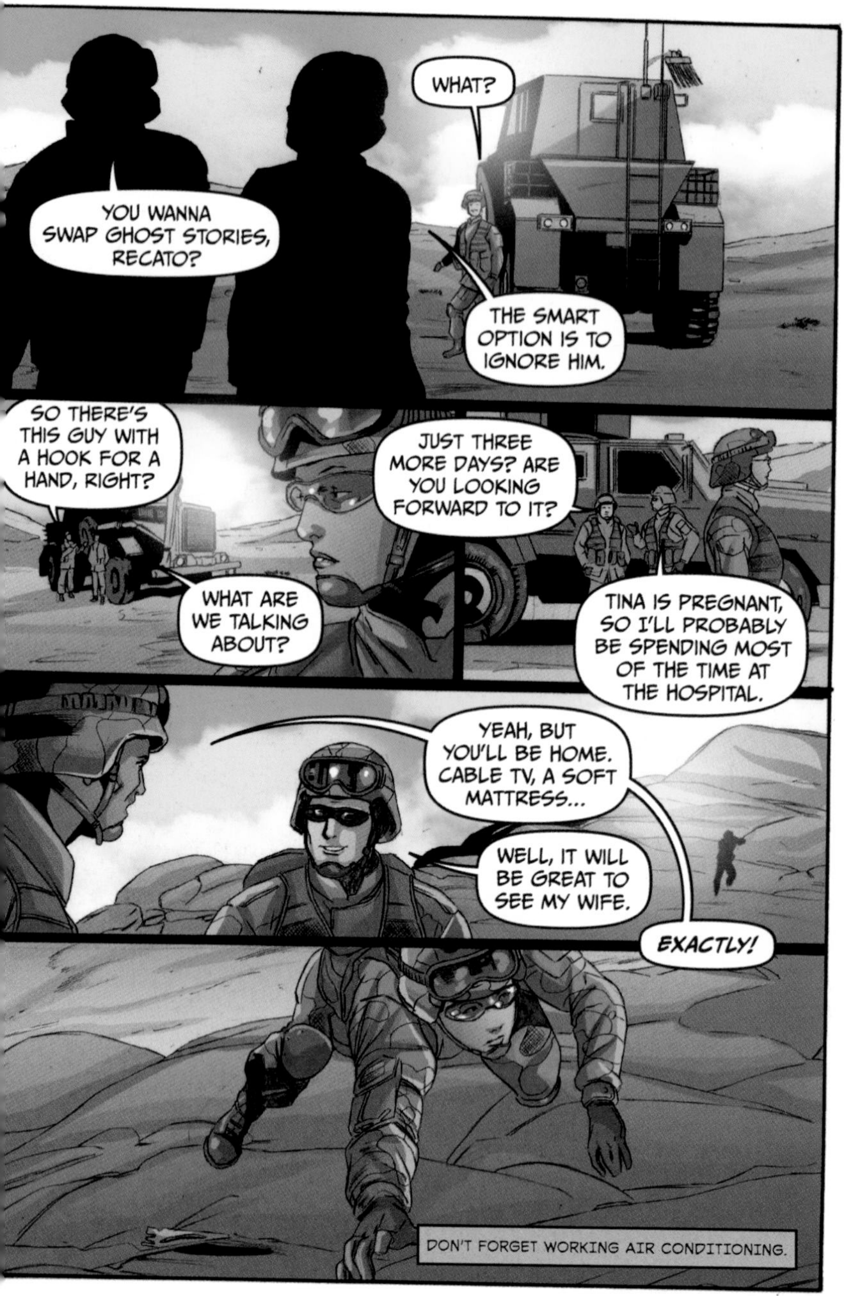
YOU WANNA SWAP GHOST STORIES, RECATO?
WHAT?
THE SMART OPTION IS TO IGNORE HIM.
SO THERE'S THIS GUY WITH A HOOK FOR A HAND, RIGHT?
WHAT ARE WE TALKING ABOUT?
JUST THREE MORE DAYS? ARE YOU LOOKING FORWARD TO IT?
TINA IS PREGNANT, SO I'LL PROBABLY BE SPENDING MOST OF THE TIME AT THE HOSPITAL.
YEAH, BUT YOU'LL BE HOME. CABLE TV, A SOFT MATTRESS...
WELL, IT WILL BE GREAT TO SEE MY WIFE.
EXACTLY!
DON'T FORGET WORKING AIR CONDITIONING.

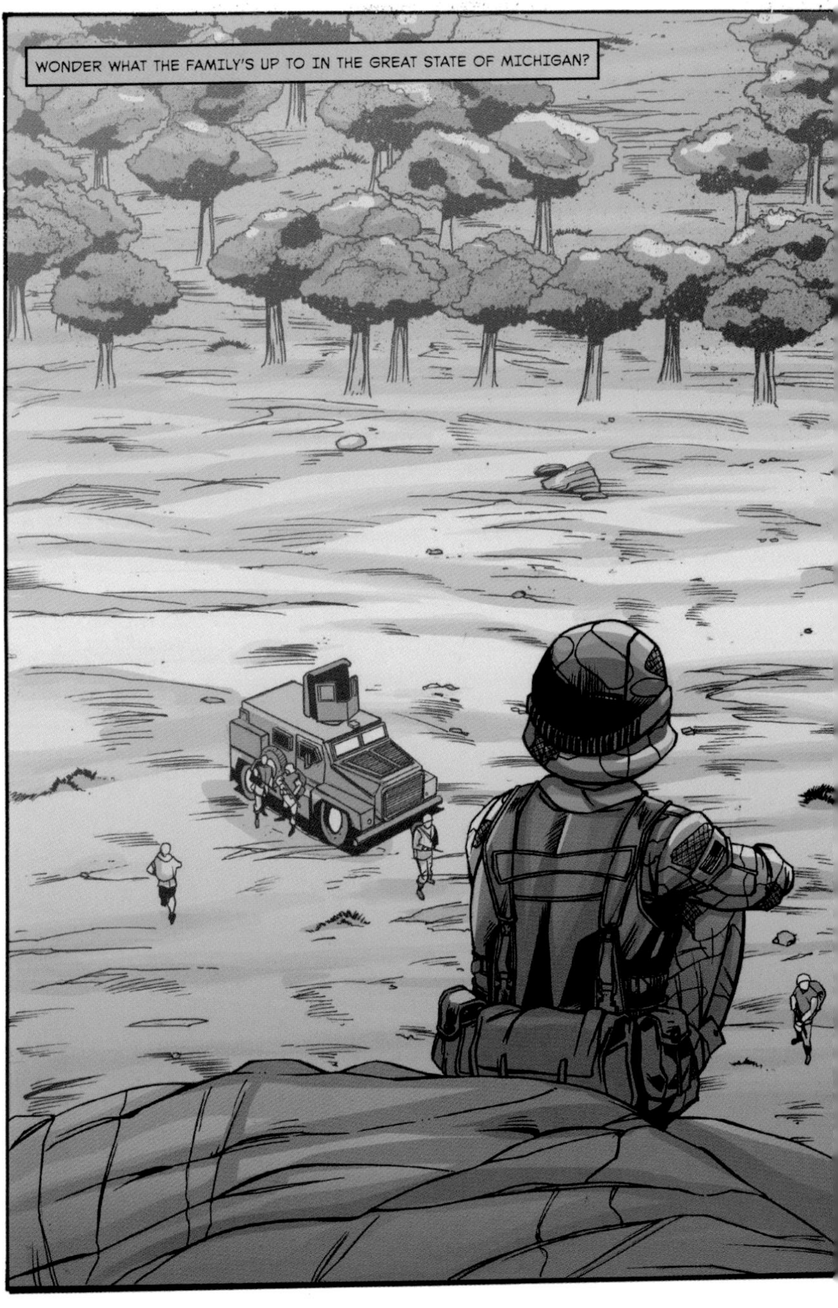
WONDER WHAT THE FAMILY'S UP TO IN THE GREAT STATE OF MICHIGAN?

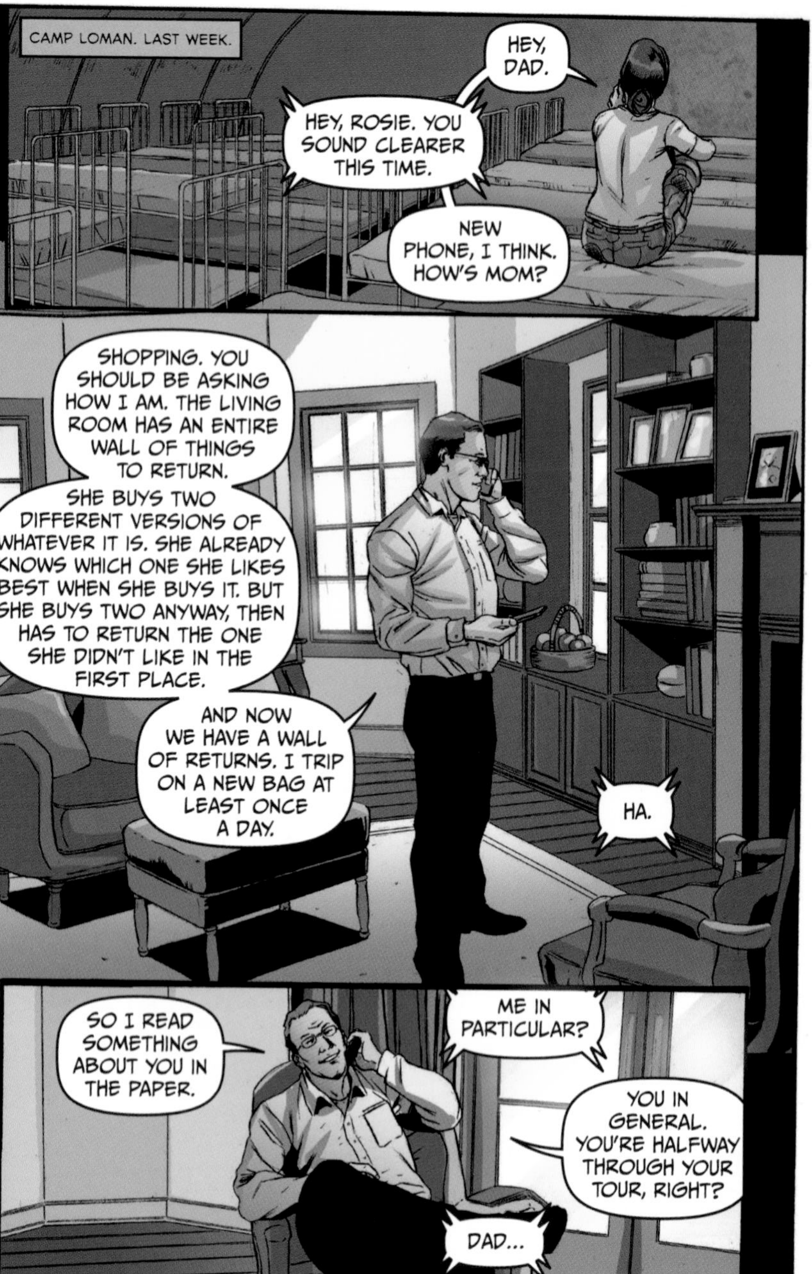
CAMP LOMAN. LAST WEEK.
HEY, DAD.
HEY, ROSIE. YOU SOUND CLEARER THIS TIME.
NEW PHONE, I THINK. HOW'S MOM?
SHOPPING. YOU SHOULD BE ASKING HOW I AM. THE LIVING ROOM HAS AN ENTIRE WALL OF THINGS TO RETURN.
SHE BUYS TWO DIFFERENT VERSIONS OF WHATEVER IT IS. SHE ALREADY KNOWS WHICH ONE SHE LIKES BEST WHEN SHE BUYS IT. BUT SHE BUYS TWO ANYWAY, THEN HAS TO RETURN THE ONE SHE DIDN'T LIKE IN THE FIRST PLACE.
AND NOW WE HAVE A WALL OF RETURNS. I TRIP ON A NEW BAG AT LEAST ONCE A DAY.
HA.
SO I READ SOMETHING ABOUT YOU IN THE PAPER.
ME IN PARTICULAR?
YOU IN GENERAL. YOU'RE HALFWAY THROUGH YOUR TOUR, RIGHT?
DAD...

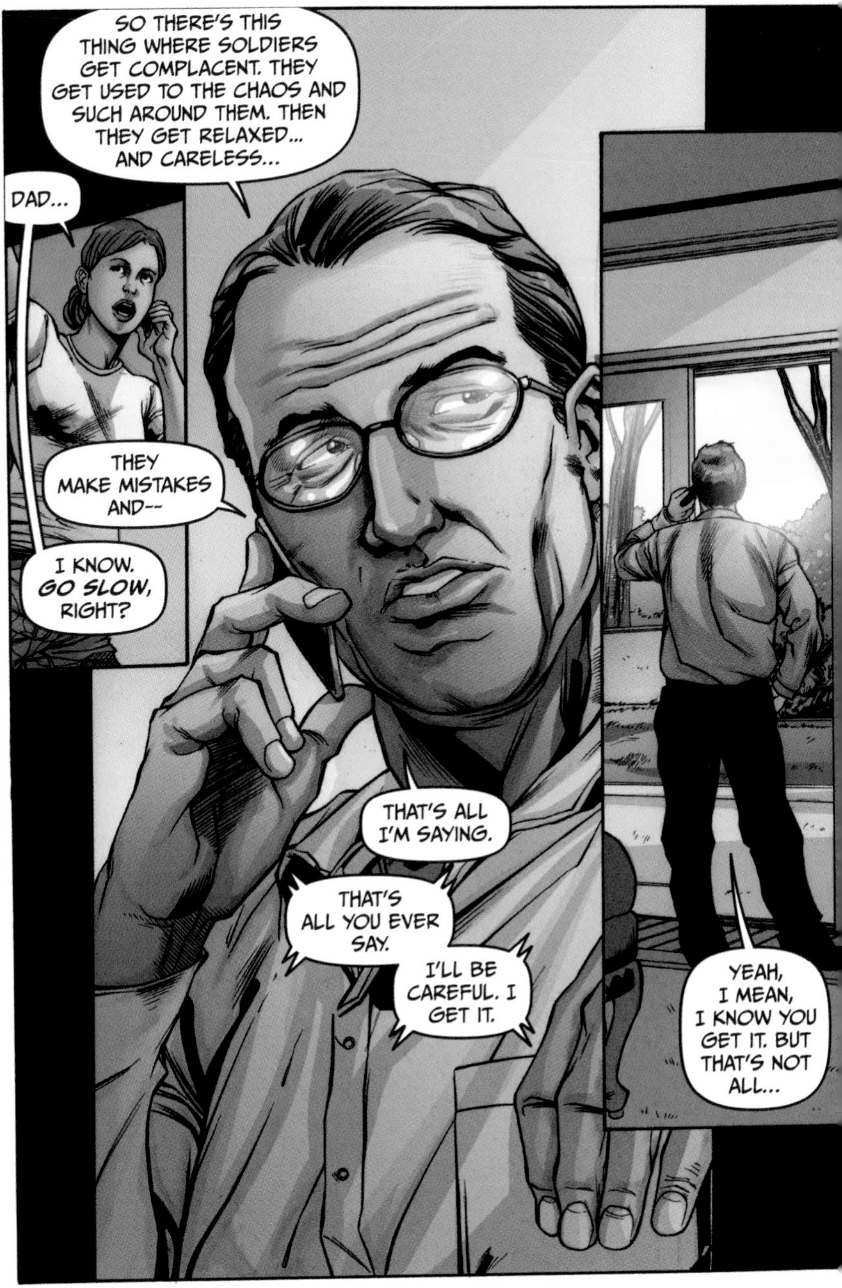
SO THERE'S THIS THING WHERE SOLDIERS GET COMPLACENT. THEY GET USED TO THE CHAOS AND SUCH AROUND THEM. THEN THEY GET RELAXED... AND CARELESS...
DAD...
THEY MAKE MISTAKES AND--
I KNOW. *GO SLOW,* RIGHT?
THAT'S ALL I'M SAYING.
THAT'S ALL YOU EVER SAY.
I'LL BE CAREFUL. I GET IT.
YEAH, I MEAN, I KNOW YOU GET IT. BUT THAT'S NOT ALL...

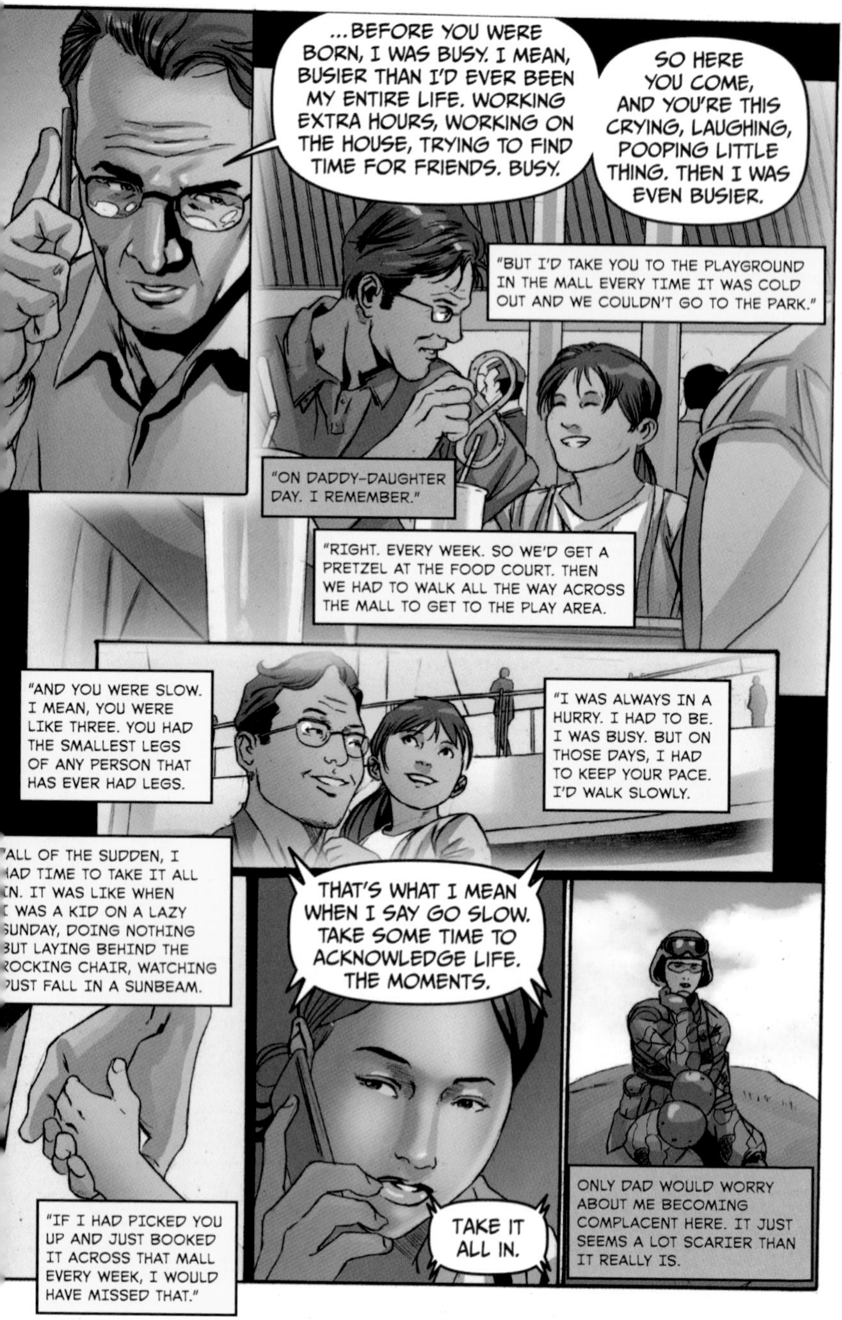
...BEFORE YOU WERE BORN, I WAS BUSY. I MEAN, BUSIER THAN I'D EVER BEEN MY ENTIRE LIFE. WORKING EXTRA HOURS, WORKING ON THE HOUSE, TRYING TO FIND TIME FOR FRIENDS. BUSY.
SO HERE YOU COME, AND YOU'RE THIS CRYING, LAUGHING, POOPING LITTLE THING. THEN I WAS EVEN BUSIER.
"BUT I'D TAKE YOU TO THE PLAYGROUND IN THE MALL EVERY TIME IT WAS COLD OUT AND WE COULDN'T GO TO THE PARK."
"ON DADDY-DAUGHTER DAY. I REMEMBER."
"RIGHT. EVERY WEEK. SO WE'D GET A PRETZEL AT THE FOOD COURT. THEN WE HAD TO WALK ALL THE WAY ACROSS THE MALL TO GET TO THE PLAY AREA.
"AND YOU WERE SLOW. I MEAN, YOU WERE LIKE THREE. YOU HAD THE SMALLEST LEGS OF ANY PERSON THAT HAS EVER HAD LEGS.
"I WAS ALWAYS IN A HURRY. I HAD TO BE. I WAS BUSY. BUT ON THOSE DAYS, I HAD TO KEEP YOUR PACE. I'D WALK SLOWLY.
ALL OF THE SUDDEN, I HAD TIME TO TAKE IT ALL IN. IT WAS LIKE WHEN I WAS A KID ON A LAZY SUNDAY, DOING NOTHING BUT LAYING BEHIND THE ROCKING CHAIR, WATCHING DUST FALL IN A SUNBEAM.
"IF I HAD PICKED YOU UP AND JUST BOOKED IT ACROSS THAT MALL EVERY WEEK, I WOULD HAVE MISSED THAT."
THAT'S WHAT I MEAN WHEN I SAY GO SLOW. TAKE SOME TIME TO ACKNOWLEDGE LIFE. THE MOMENTS.
TAKE IT ALL IN.
ONLY DAD WOULD WORRY ABOUT ME BECOMING COMPLACENT HERE. IT JUST SEEMS A LOT SCARIER THAN IT REALLY IS.

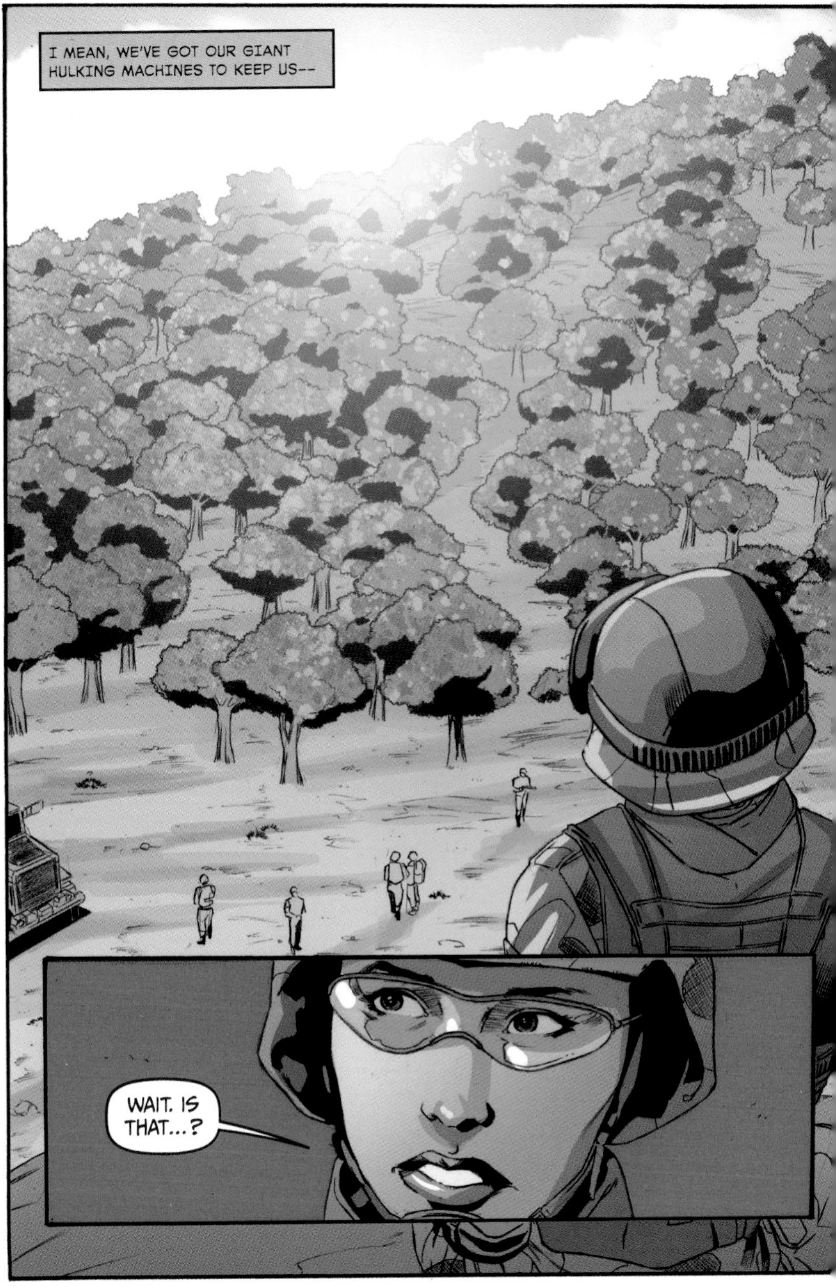
I MEAN, WE'VE GOT OUR GIANT HULKING MACHINES TO KEEP US--
WAIT. IS THAT...?

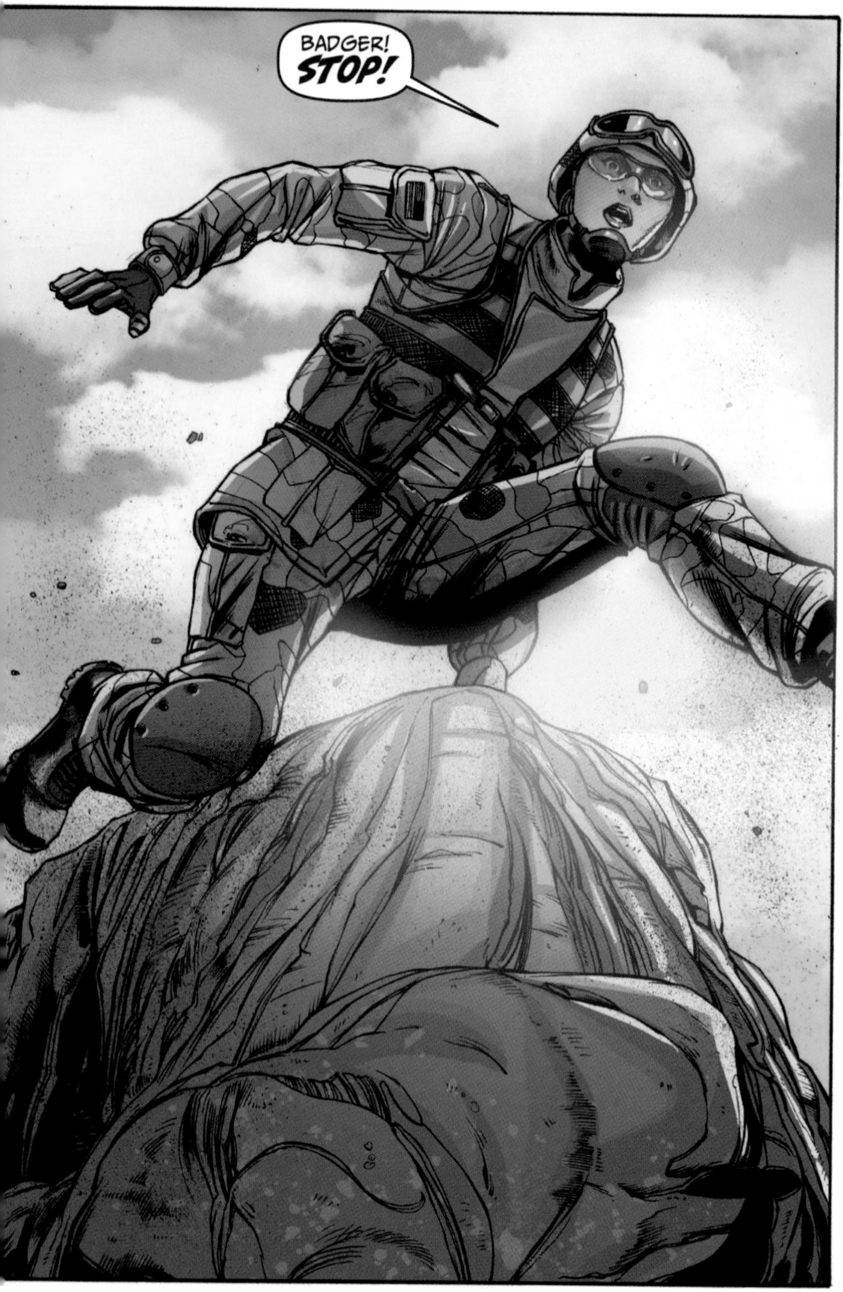
BADGER! STOP!

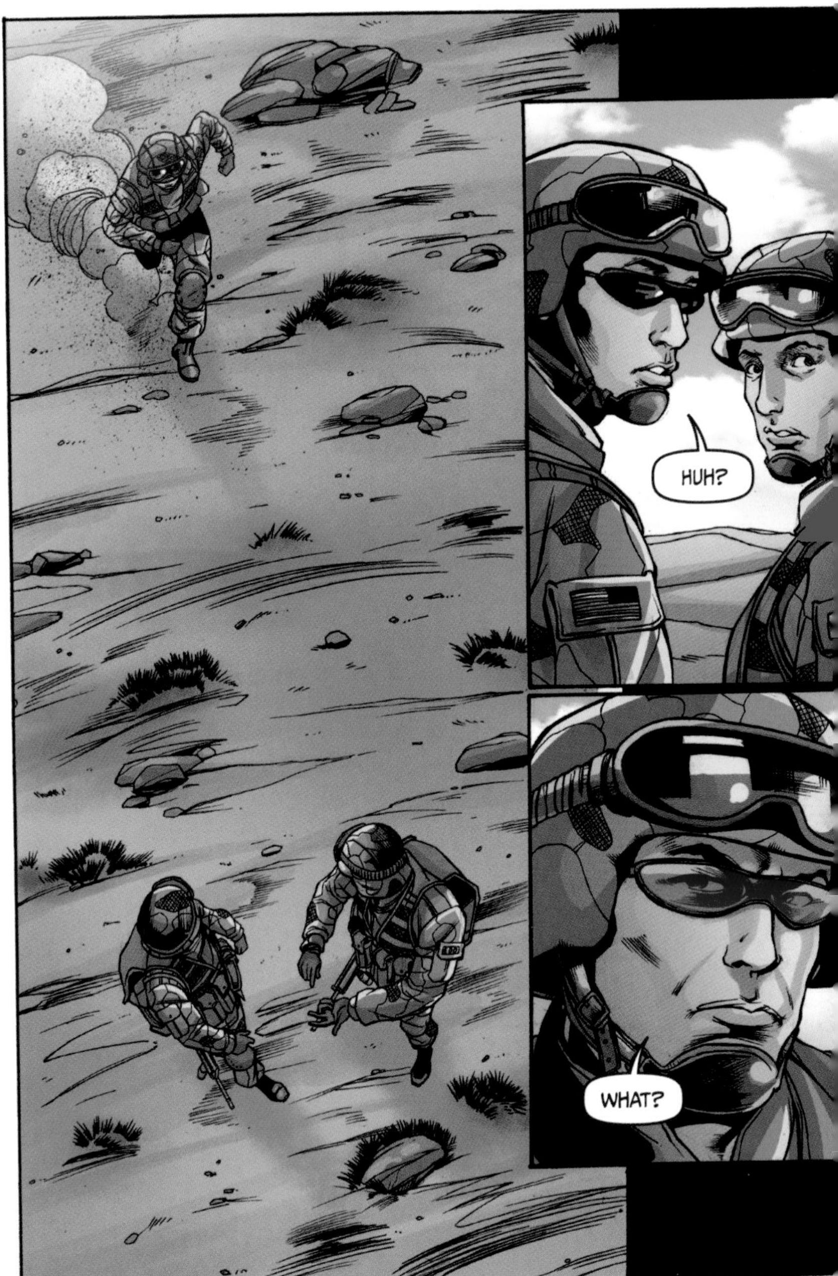
HUH?
WHAT?

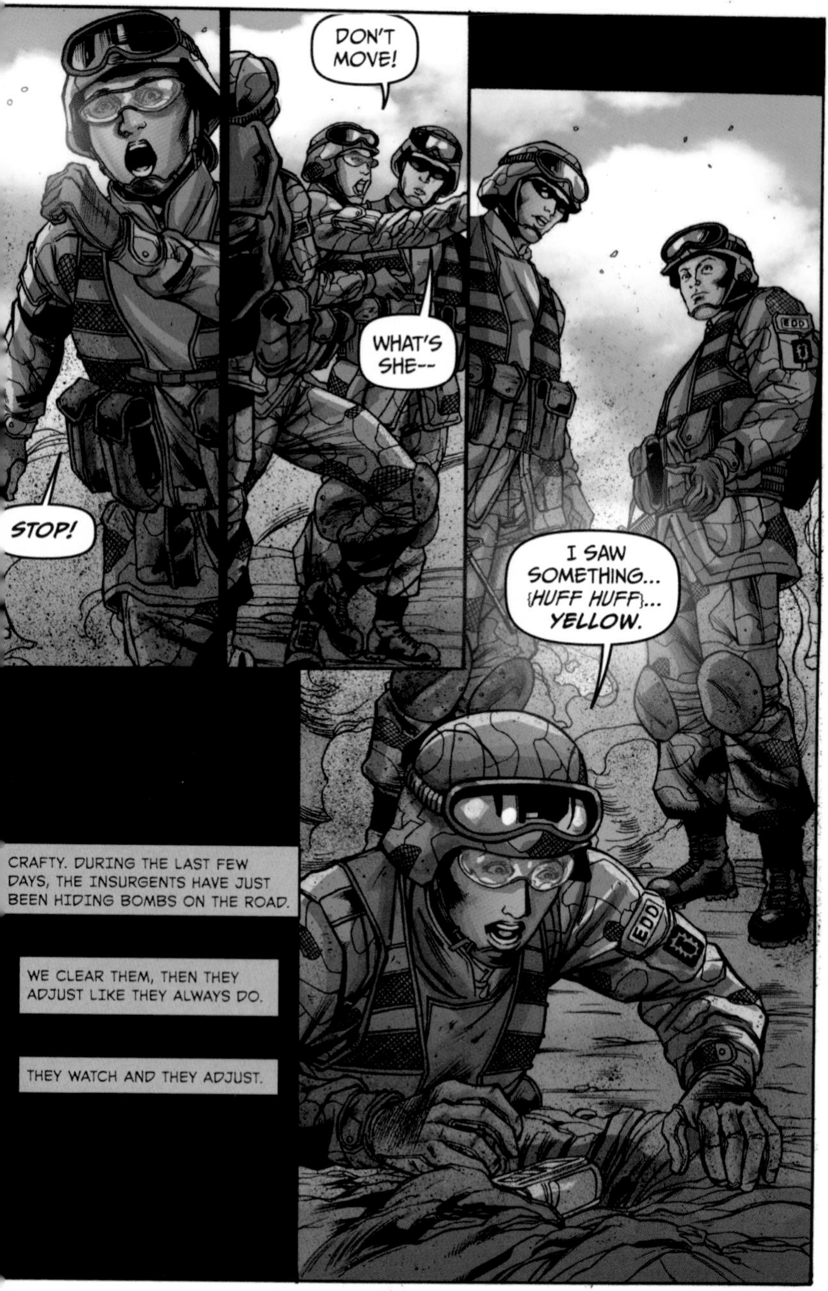
STOP!
DON'T MOVE!
WHAT'S SHE--
I SAW SOMETHING... {HUFF HUFF}... YELLOW.
CRAFTY. DURING THE LAST FEW DAYS, THE INSURGENTS HAVE JUST BEEN HIDING BOMBS ON THE ROAD.
WE CLEAR THEM, THEN THEY ADJUST LIKE THEY ALWAYS DO.
THEY WATCH AND THEY ADJUST.

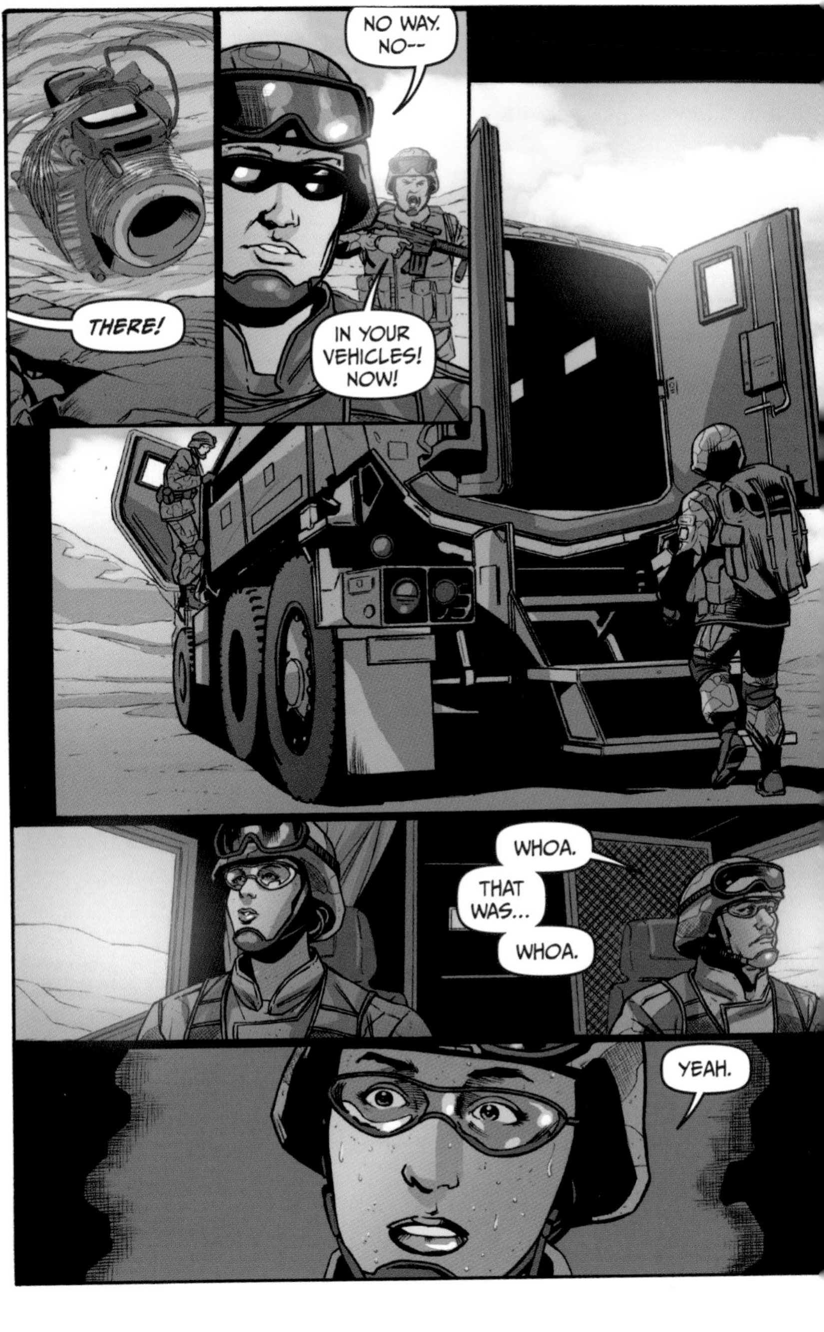
NO WAY. NO--
THERE!
IN YOUR VEHICLES! NOW!
WHOA.
THAT WAS...
WHOA.
YEAH.

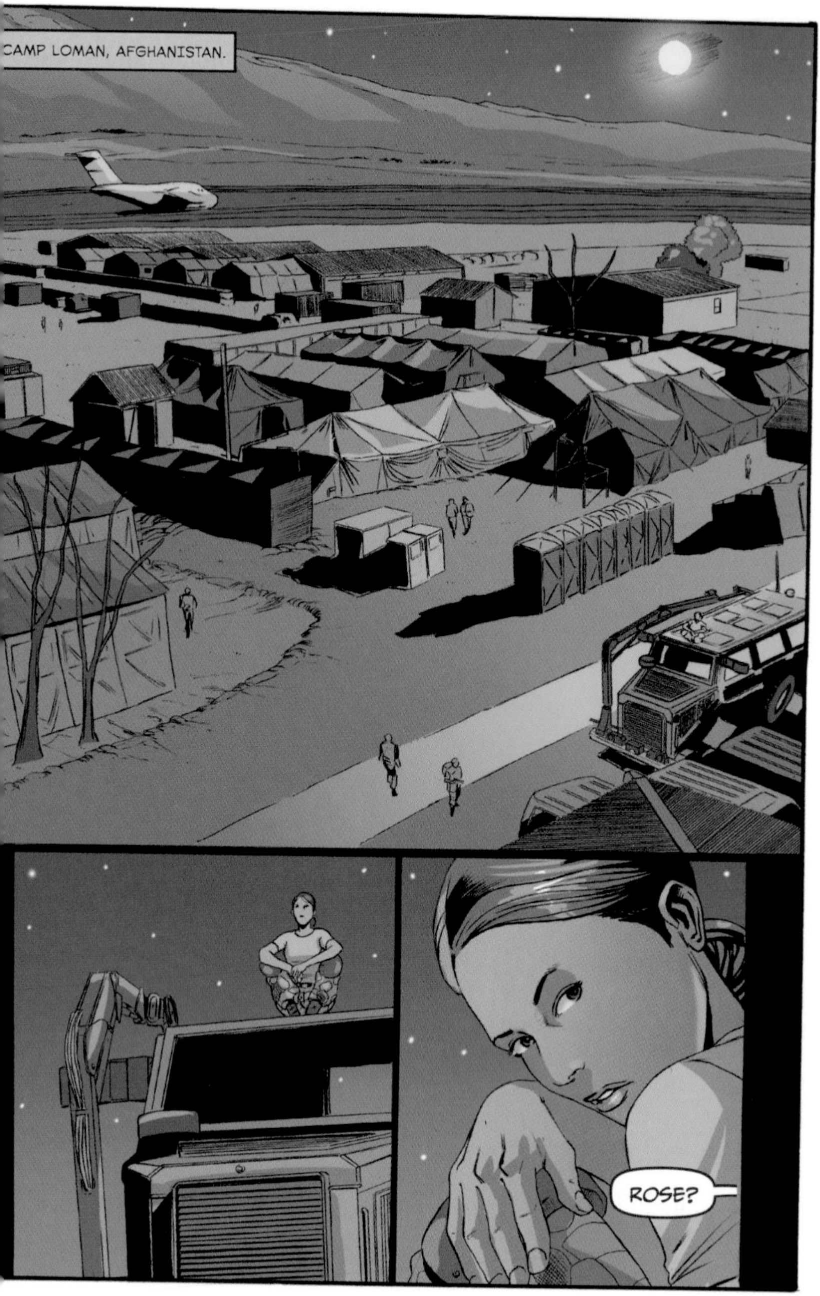
CAMP LOMAN, AFGHANISTAN.
ROSE?

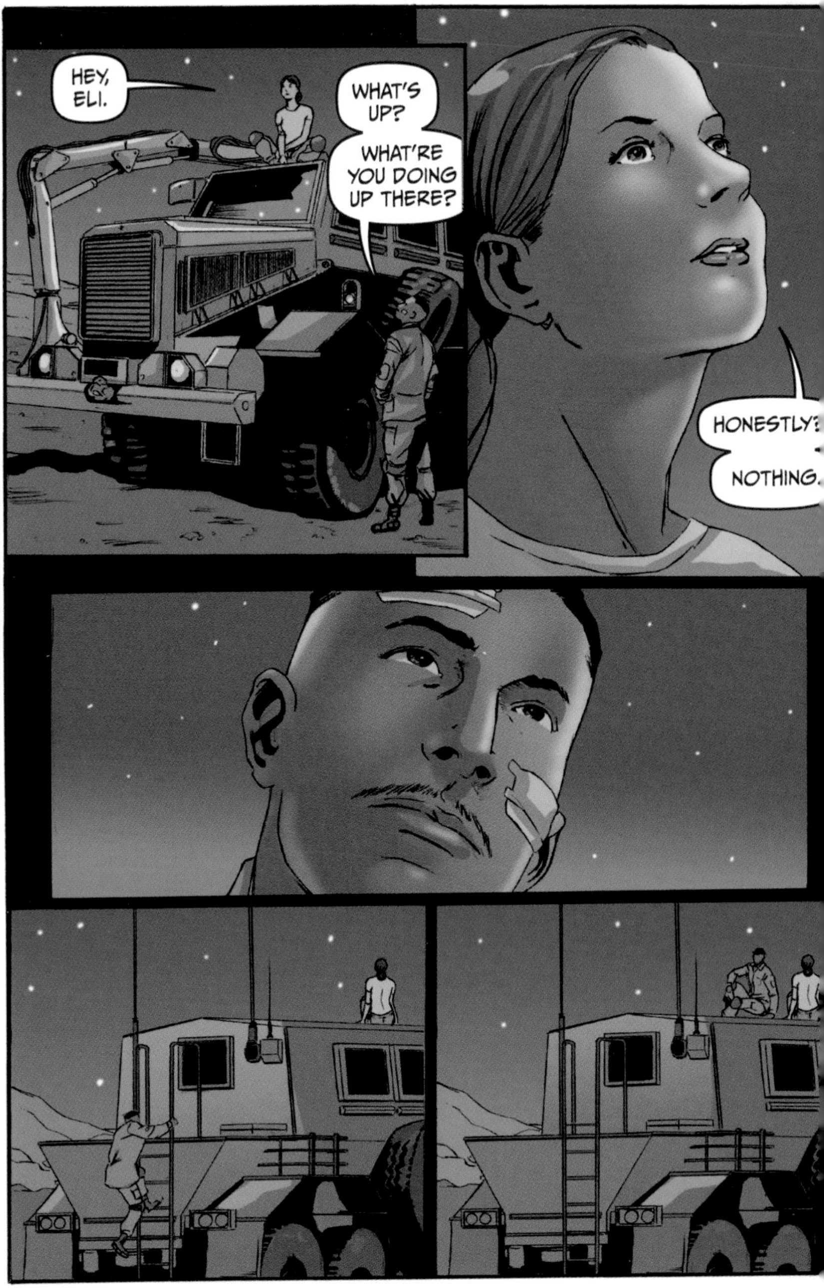
HEY, ELI.
WHAT'S UP?
WHAT'RE YOU DOING UP THERE?
HONESTLY?
NOTHING.

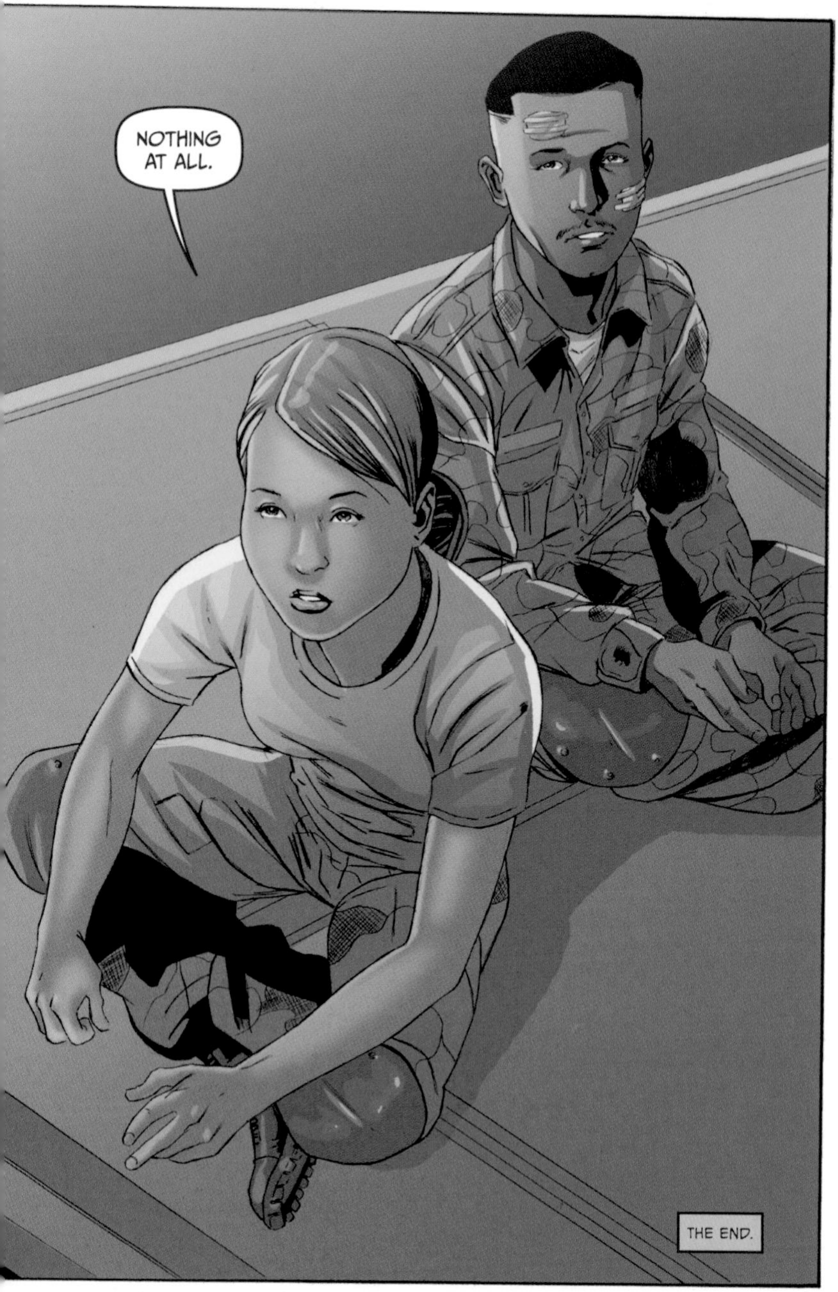
NOTHING AT ALL.
THE END.

EOD SOLDIERS

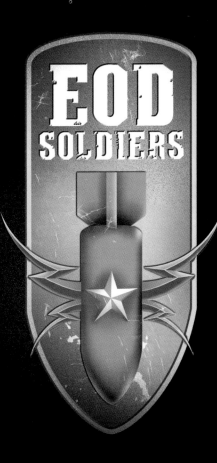

★ EOD BADGE ★

All Explosive Ordnance Disposal (EOD) soldiers and sailors can be identified by the badge on their uniforms. The EOD Badge is made up of a wreath, a bomb, two lightning bolts, and a shield. Each of these objects has special meaning:

WREATH

The wreath represents the awards given to service members who reduce the potential for accidents through their ingenuity and devotion to their duty. It also honors the memory of EOD members who have sacrificed their lives while doing their job.

BOMB

The bomb represents the unexploded bomb at the center of every EOD mission. Its three fins stand for nuclear, conventional, and chemical and biological warfare. The look of the bomb is taken from the original Bomb Disposal Badge awarded during World War II (1939-1945).

LIGHTNING BOLTS

The lightning bolts represent the destructive power of a bomb and the courage of EOD service members. They also stand for the professional manner in which EOD service members strive to reduce hazards and make explosive devices harmless.

SHIELD

The shield stands for an EOD service member's mission to protect people and property from the accidental detonation of an unexploded bomb.

The design of the EOD Badge dates back to the 1950s. Today it is issued at three levels—the Basic EOD Badge, the Senior EOD Badge, and the Master EOD Badge. Each of these badges looks the same for all branches of the military.

VISUAL QUESTIONS

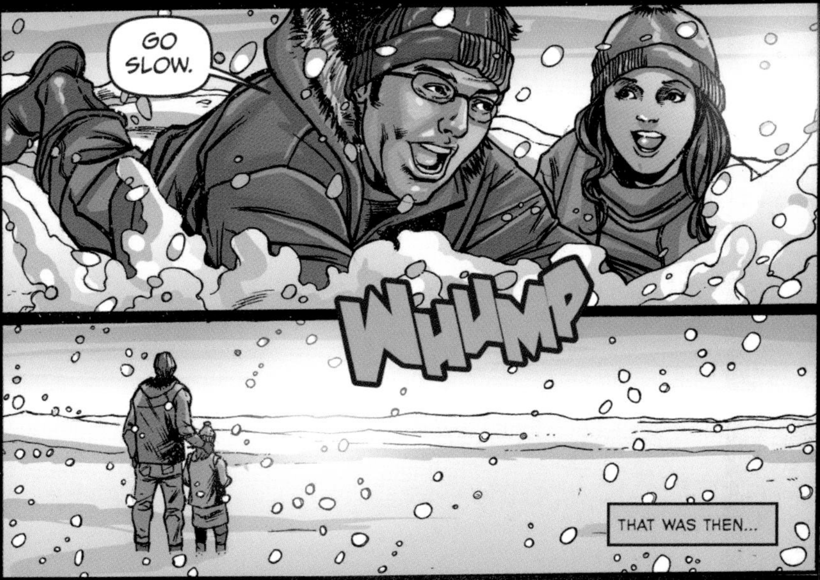
GO SLOW.
WHUMP
THAT WAS THEN...

1. Why does Rose's father dive into the snow after she falls, but then tell her to go slow? How is his advice important to the whole story?

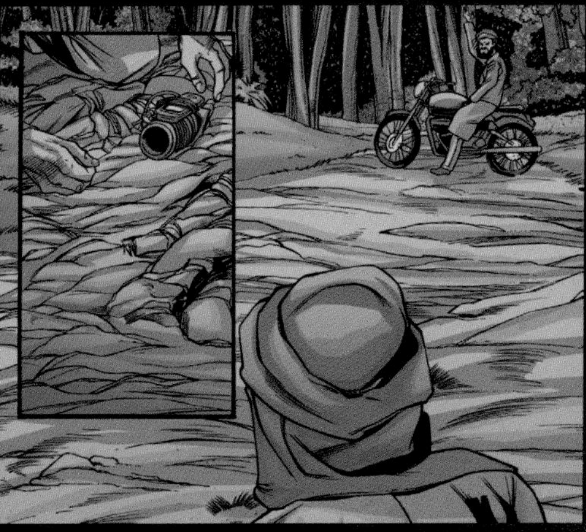

2. These two panels don't use any narrative or dialogue. What is happening in the small inset panel? Why is the man on the motorcycle waving? What information do these scenes give you without any words at all?

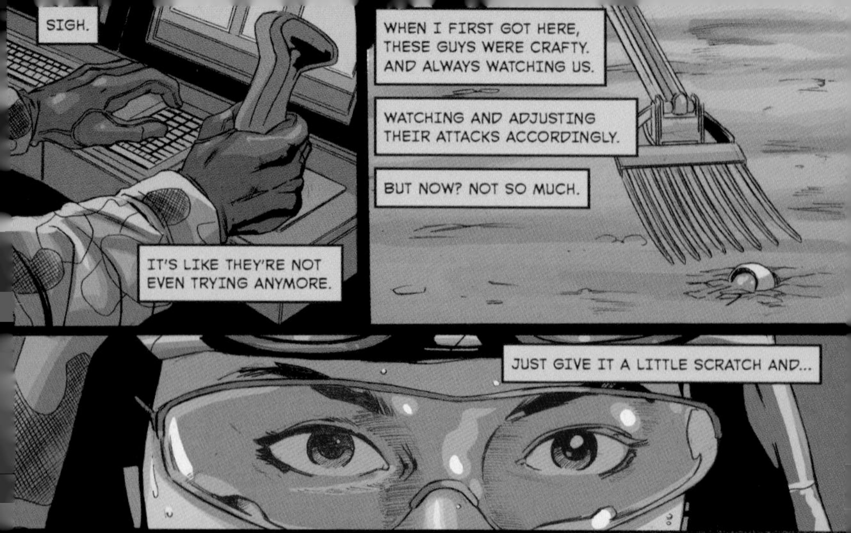
SIGH.
IT'S LIKE THEY'RE NOT EVEN TRYING ANYMORE.
WHEN I FIRST GOT HERE, THESE GUYS WERE CRAFTY. AND ALWAYS WATCHING US.
WATCHING AND ADJUSTING THEIR ATTACKS ACCORDINGLY.
BUT NOW? NOT SO MUCH.
JUST GIVE IT A LITTLE SCRATCH AND...

3. Graphic novels build tension with a combination of words and art. How do these three panels, and the narrative boxes that go with them, build tension in this story? Which panel is the most intense and why?

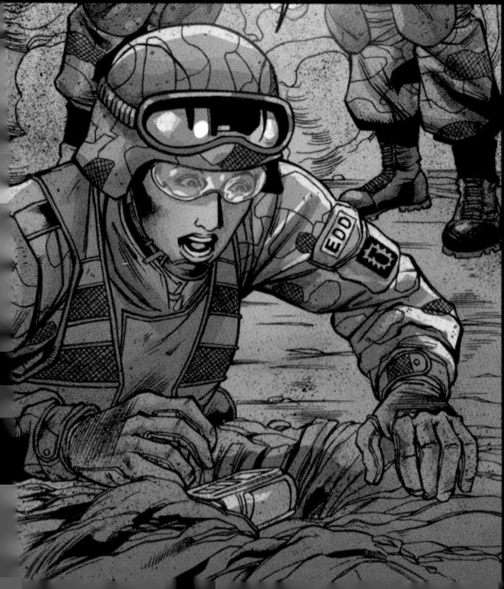
EDD

4. Facial expressions can tell you a lot about how a character is feeling and what she is thinking. What does Rose's expression tel you about how she feels right now. What types of thoughts might be going through her mind?

AUTHOR

Matthew K. Manning is the author of more than 40 books and dozens of comic books. His work ranges from the Amazon top-selling hardcover, *Batman: A Visual History*, to the children's book, *Superman: An Origin Story*, to a series of graphic novels featuring the military's bomb squad in Afghanistan. Over the course of his career, he has written books starring Batman, Superman, Spider-Man, Wolverine, the Joker, Scooby-Doo, Iron Man, Wonder Woman, Flash, Thor, Green Lantern, Captain America, the Hulk, Harley Quinn, and the Avengers. Currently one of the regular writers for IDW's comic series *Teenage Mutant Ninja Turtles: Amazing Adventures*, Manning has also written for several other comic book titles, including serving as one of the regular writers for *Beware the Batman*, *The Batman Strikes!*, *Legion of Super-Heroes in the 31st Century*, and *Teenage Mutant Ninja Turtles: New Animated Adventures*. He lives in Asheville, North Carolina, with his wife, Dorothy, and his two daughters, Lillian and Gwendolyn.

GLOSSARY

biological warfare (bye-oh-LOJ-i-kuhl WOR-fair)—having to do with germs, sickness caused by germs, or germ weapons

complacent (kuhm-PLAY-suhnt)—overconfident and unconcerned with the actual dangers around oneself

conventional (kuhn-VEN-shuh-nuhl)—something that is traditional or standard

devotion (di-VOH-shuhn)—the act of giving your time, effort, or attention to some purpose

dismount (DIS-maunt)—to get down from, or off of, something

IED (EYE-EE-DEE)—stands for Improvised Explosive Device; a homemade bomb often made with material not usually found in bombs

ingenuity (in-ji-NOO-i-tee)—being inventive and original

insurgent (in-SUR-juhnt)—a person who rebels and fights against his or her country's ruling government and those who support it

interrogate (in-TER-uh-gate)—to question someone in detail or determine the nature of a suspected bomb

lieutenant (loo-TEN-uhnt)—a rank in the U.S. military above sergeant and below captain

sacrifice (SAK-ruh-fise)—give something up for the good of others

MORE EOD SOLDIERS

EOD SOLDIERS
TWO SIDES
MANNING
FURUZONO
LIMA

EOD SOLDIERS
THE MIST
MANNING
FURUZONO
LIMA

EOD SOLDIERS
THE LIST
MANNING
FURUZONO
LIMA

EOD SOLDIERS
GO SLOW
MANNING
FURUZONO
LIMA

Find cool websites and more books like this one at www.facthound.com

Just type in the Book ID:
9781496531094
and you are ready to go!

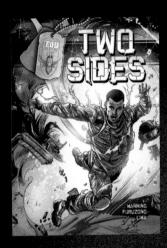